Steven tried to keep from shouting. "So let me get this straight . . . since you're entering the guitar competition, you hope to win it. Right? And if you win, you'll be moving to Spain. Right? And if you move to Spain, then obviously we're no longer together."

"Steven," Billie began with a catch in her voice.

"Right?" he repeated in a savage tone. "Answer me, Billie."

"This is my life. *My* life, Steven. Meaning it belongs to me. Billie Winkler. And *I* get to make some decisions about it," she shouted at the top of her voice.

Billie stood in front of Steven, red-faced with fury, tears of anger streaming down her cheeks. "So this is about you making a decision about breaking up and—"

"Who said anything about breaking up?" she yelled.

He stared at her. "You're talking about leaving me," he said in a slow, patient tone. "If you're on one continent and I'm on another, it's kind of hard to maintain a relationship."

"I knew you were going to react like this," she said angrily, reaching into her pocket for a tissue. "I can't talk to you about anything anymore."

"I'm out of here," Steven announced as he stormed out of their apartment.

Bantam Books in the Sweet Valley University series
Ask your bookseller for the books you have missed

And don't miss these
Sweet Valley University Thriller Editions:

# SWEET VALLEY UNIVERSITY®

# Billie's Secret

### Written by
### Laurie John

### Created by
### FRANCINE PASCAL

BANTAM BOOKS
NEW YORK · TORONTO · LONDON · SYDNEY · AUCKLAND

RL 6, age 12 and up

BILLIE'S SECRET

*A Bantam Book / February 1996*

*Sweet Valley High® and Sweet Valley University®*
*are registered trademarks of Francine Pascal*
*Conceived by Francine Pascal*
*Produced by Daniel Weiss Associates, Inc.*
*33 West 17th Street*
*New York, NY 10011*

ISBN: 0-553-56699-7

*Published simultaneously in the United States and Canada*

*Bantam Books are published by Bantam Books, a division of Bantam*
*Doubleday Dell Publishing Group, Inc. Its trademark, consisting of the*
*words "Bantam Books" and the portrayal of a rooster, is Registered in*
*U.S. Patent and Trademark Office and in other countries. Marca*
*Registrada. Bantam Books, 1540 Broadway, New York, New York 10036.*

PRINTED IN THE UNITED STATES OF AMERICA

OPM    0  9  8  7  6  5  4  3  2  1

*To Matthew Pascal*

# Chapter One

"I am *not*!" Elizabeth Wakefield shouted.

Her denial was followed by a raucous shout of laughter from everybody else at the table.

"You are too," Elizabeth's twin sister, Jessica, accused with a laugh. "You're the biggest busybody on the Sweet Valley University campus."

"That's what makes her a great broadcast journalist," Tom Watts said, reaching for the salad. He helped himself to another generous portion of thick-sliced tomatoes and avocado.

"And you're the *second*-biggest busybody," Jessica added, pointing a manicured fingernail at Tom.

Tom laughed so hard he almost dropped the salad bowl.

Steven Wakefield sat back in his chair, feeling more deeply satisfied than he had in a long time. Life was good. For once, life seemed to be running smoothly—not just for him and his girlfriend,

1

Billie, but also for his sister Elizabeth and her boy-friend, Tom Watts.

For Steven, the best part of the dinner party was seeing his sister Jessica smile and laugh. It had been a long time since he'd seen a genuine smile on Jessica's face. He'd been worried about her. More worried than he liked to admit.

Jessica was only eighteen. But she'd experienced more romantic disasters in those eighteen years than most people experienced in a lifetime. Most recently, she'd had a love affair with a young professor, Louis Miles. The affair had gone tragically wrong when Cloe, his insane ex-wife, had pursued Jessica and Louis through Arizona, New Mexico, and Colorado.

Eventually, in an effort to protect Jessica from his ex-wife's determination to kill her, Louis had driven Cloe, and himself, over a cliff.

The loss of Louis had left Jessica uncharacteristically quiet and withdrawn, in a state of numb grief from which she was just now beginning to emerge. Steven, Billie, Elizabeth, and Tom had all tried to spend as much time with her as they could.

Gradually Jessica was coming back. Becoming a little more like her old self. But she still had a long way to go.

Steven and Billie had actually planned tonight's dinner party in an effort to get Jessica out of the dorm room she shared with Elizabeth . . . to cheer her up. They'd given a lot of thought to the

2

menu, making sure they had all of Jessica's favorite foods. Steven had even bought an arrangement of Jessica's favorite flowers. Orchids. Pale and delicately scented. He'd placed the flowers in the center of the round pine dining-room table. Their porcelain colors blended beautifully with the soft tones of Billie and Steven's apartment.

When Jessica left, Steven planned to give her the flowers. They'd make any room look cheerful.

"Steven, these barbecued veggies are great," Tom commented, reaching for the large Mexican-style serving platter. "How did you make them?"

"It's an ancient family secret," Steven answered, picking up his fork.

"A family secret called salt and pepper," Billie said, giving him a teasing poke in the ribs.

"Bigmouth," Steven scolded in mock anger.

The table erupted into laughter again, and Steven joined in. He liked hearing the sound of laughter and conversation in the apartment he and Billie shared. And he enjoyed feeling as if he and Billie were already a family.

Steven and Billie had been living together for two years. They both had two more years before they graduated from SVU. For them, love had been easy. And Steven knew she was the woman he wanted to spend the rest of his life with.

"Isn't that so, Steven?"

Steven blinked, realizing that the conversation had moved on without him. "Sorry," he said to Billie. "I was daydreaming. What was the question?"

3

"We were talking about the future. How soon is too soon to start making plans?"

Steven put down his fork. This was a subject he could really get into. "It's never too soon to start. The sooner you focus on what you want out of life, the better your chances are of getting it."

Tom nodded. "Yeah. But don't you think people need to try out different things? It's easy to get off on the wrong foot and wind up pursuing something that's not right for you. I started college thinking life was all football. I found out that broadcast journalism is a lot more interesting. What if I'd stuck with football and then found out too late that it wasn't for me?"

"Well, sure," Steven agreed. "You have to keep an open mind. But . . . if you know where your talents and interests lie, why not go ahead and start making your dreams happen? Look at me and Billie. We know exactly what we want. We want to be together as much as possible. We want economic security for ourselves and our children. And we want to be lawyers. So after we graduate from law school, we'll open our own practice and work together, help each other, combine child rearing and office duties. We'll get the most out of life."

"Sounds like you've got it all figured out," Jessica said with a wistful smile.

"Nobody's got it *all* figured out," Tom said kindly. He reached over and squeezed her hand.

Steven felt a flicker of guilt. He and Elizabeth were both directed, academically disciplined, and

4

good self-starters. But Jessica was floundering helplessly. There was no sense rubbing it in and making her feel bad. He was supposed to be cheering her up.

Being a good brother to the twins wasn't always an easy job. Even though the girls looked exactly alike, with their long blond hair and blue-green eyes, they were very different people. And they needed different things from him.

Elizabeth was a good student with a serious interest in broadcast journalism. Steven tended to treat her more as an equal than Jessica.

Jessica was extremely intelligent. But she was also emotional, impulsive, and in desperate need of a direction.

"Tom's right," Steven said quickly, trying to make Jessica feel better about herself. "For some people, it's better to move slowly through school. Be flexible and take your time about making choices."

"Speaking of choices," Billie said, gracefully changing the subject. "Let's talk about dessert. Chocolate mousse cake or lemon-vanilla crunch?"

Steven threw her a grateful smile and she smiled back, giving him an almost imperceptible wink. They made a good team, he and Billie. No doubt about it—Steven Wakefield was a lucky man. Billie Winkler was beautiful, smart, capable. Everything he wanted in a life partner.

Steven stood and began clearing the table while Billie found out what everyone wanted for dessert.

Steven carried an armload of plates through the swinging door that closed the small kitchen off from the dining- and living-room area. He let the door swing shut behind him and began scraping the remains of dinner into the garbage. A few minutes later Billie materialized at his elbow.

"Thanks for changing the subject," he said softly as Billie reached up to get the dessert bowls out of the cabinet. He leaned over and kissed her cheek. "And thank you for being so nice to my sisters."

"It's no big deal," she responded in an amused voice. "I like your sisters."

"They like you too," he said, feeling as completely happy as it was possible for a man to feel. He rinsed his hands, dried them, and then pulled Billie gently toward him. He wrapped his arms around her waist, sneaking a kiss before it was time to rejoin their guests.

Jessica scraped the last bit of lemon-vanilla crunch from the bottom of her dessert bowl. She put the spoon in her mouth and let the cool, tangy dessert melt on the back of her tongue while she listened to Elizabeth, Billie, and Tom wrap up an intense political debate.

"Statistics can be made to prove anything," Tom informed Billie in a heated and exasperated tone. "Why do lawyers always throw statistics around when they *know* they're meaningless? It's such an exercise in truth manipulation!"

Billie let out an outraged snort. "*A*—I'm not a lawyer yet. And *B*—if you want to talk about manipulating the truth, the news media is notorious for—"

"Hold it! Hold it!" Elizabeth interrupted. She held up her hand and demanded the floor. "I get so tired of hearing people bash the media . . ."

"They *deserve* bashing," Billie insisted.

Tom made a dissenting noise, and then he and Billie began talking at once, arguing in loud voices. Elizabeth quickly tapped on her glass with a spoon, trying to get them to let her talk.

They were having a great time, but political debates weren't Jessica's idea of fun. She took her bowl and went into the kitchen, where Steven was doing some last-minute cleanup at the sink—attacking a cast-iron pot with a pad of steel wool.

"Hi," he said with a smile. "Back for more dessert?"

She shook her head and put her bowl down on the counter. "Nope. I've had all I can hold."

He went back to his pot scrubbing, and she leaned against the counter and sighed.

"That's not a happy sound," Steven said, putting the pot down in the sink. Holding his wet, soapy hands away from her silk blouse, Steven put an arm around her and gave her a big-brotherly hug. "It's going to be all right, Jessica," he promised. "I know you don't think so, but it will."

The lump that had been lurking in the base of Jessica's throat rose up, and her eyes filled with tears. "What's the matter with me?" she choked. "Louis is gone. He's dead. But I can't forget him. I can't stop loving him. And I can't stop hurting. I don't know what to do."

Steven tightened his grip around her shoulders. "You've just got to hang on."

"To what?" she asked. "I'm not like you and Elizabeth. I've never been good in school."

"You've made straight A's more than once," he reminded her. He released her shoulders and handed her a paper napkin to blow her nose on.

"Okay. I guess I can be a good student. When I'm interested. But most of the time I'm not."

Steven tightened his lips but said nothing, and Jessica was grateful. He'd delivered a million lectures to her on the importance of education. She knew he was right, but for whatever reason, it didn't seem to affect the way she lived her life.

Jessica's route just wasn't going to be as easy as his and Elizabeth's. That was obvious to her now—even though she'd always thought her goals in life were simple. "I always thought . . ." She broke off and looked away.

"Always thought what?" Steven prompted.

Jessica bit her lip. Her values and ambitions were so unlike Steven's.

"You can tell me."

"It sounds stupid and corny, but I always felt like the purpose of my life was to find true love. To fall in love and get married. And I always

8

thought that the person I married would take care of me. Pretty stupid, huh?"

"It's not stupid at all," Steven argued. "In this day and age, though, it's probably a little unrealistic. But you're not alone in feeling that way. A lot of women—and men, too—think that's what life's all about. Finding somebody to marry. Finding somebody who'll take care of them."

"But I did get married. To Mike McAllery. And it was a huge mistake. He couldn't take care of me. He couldn't even take care of himself," she said bitterly.

Mike McAllery lived in Steven's apartment complex. In fact, he had the apartment directly below Steven and Billie. Jessica didn't dwell on it, but sometimes just being in Steven's complex could bring her down—remind her that she was a failure at love.

"So you learned a lesson," he said softly. "You made a mistake and moved on."

"No, I didn't. Because I kept looking for love. After Mike, there was James Montgomery. And then Randy Mason. And then . . ." Just thinking about Louis was so painful, she couldn't even finish her sentence.

"Everybody wants to be loved," Steven said softly. "There's nothing wrong with that."

"But love didn't solve any of my problems," Jessica pointed out.

"Did you think it would?" Steven asked with a laugh.

"Yes, I did. I guess I just always thought if I could find true love, everything else would fall into place after that. But when I did find true love—with Louis—well . . . my world just fell apart."

"You didn't have much time with Louis," Steven said kindly. "If you had, things might have turned out very differently. You would have had a chance to find out that love isn't always about pain and disappointment. And it's not always about romance and passion, either. Love—mature love—is about a lot of things besides romance. It's about shared goals. Shared values. A willingness to sacrifice for each other."

Jessica shook her head. "You and Billie have that. And maybe Tom and Elizabeth will someday. But it doesn't seem to be in the cards for me." She turned her gaze to Steven. "What am I supposed to be doing?" she asked. "I'm so confused."

Steven took her hand and led her over to the kitchen table. "Why don't you stop thinking about the rest of your life? Why don't you just focus on right now? You're not ready to date anybody else. And you probably won't be for a long time. School's not your favorite thing. Maybe you should get a job."

"A job?"

"Yeah. You're going to have to have some kind of career."

She couldn't help shivering slightly. The word *career* sounded so dry and dusty.

"I know you think a career is something like

10

law or working in a bank and . . ." He began to laugh.

"What's so funny?" she asked.

"You." He pointed to her face. "I can just hear your mind screaming, 'Fate worse than death. Fate worse than death.' But careers can also mean travel. Meeting interesting people. Making money."

"Money sounds good," Jessica said with a smile.

"So why not make money doing something that interests you?"

"Fine. I'll be a supermodel."

Steven laughed and picked up the newspaper classifieds that lay stacked on a wrought-iron table next to the back door, waiting to be taken out. "Let's see if there are any ads for models." He put the paper down on the table so they could both read it.

Jessica's eyes widened. "Look. There *is* an ad for models."

*"Models wanted for Kitty's Restaurant,"* Steven read out loud. *"Waitress experience a must.* I don't think that's the kind of modeling job you want," he said, blushing. "They don't really want models. They want busty girls to work as waitresses."

"Oh," Jessica said, immediately losing interest. She'd been a waitress before and hated it. And she definitely wasn't interested in working at some kind of girly club.

"Here's something!" He tapped a large ad

11

printed in bold. *"Taylor's department store is looking for sales help. Immediate hiring."*

"Taylor's," Jessica mused. "I haven't been there forever."

"Why don't you check it out?" Steven encouraged. "If you like your job, you'll probably have a pretty good chance of getting hired full time when you graduate. You could go through their buyer training program."

"What's that?"

"They'd train you to buy stuff for their store. You'd travel to New York and Paris and London and buy things for them to sell."

Jessica sat up a little straighter. Aside from acting or modeling, this was the first career choice that had ever sounded even halfway appealing. "What do I do?" she asked.

Steven pulled his chair closer. "We'll put together a resume for you tonight on my computer. It shouldn't take long. You don't have any employment history, except for that week you worked as a waitress. So it's really just a matter of listing your summer jobs, activities, and interests. Then tomorrow you'll take the resume to the store and tell them you want a part-time job."

"What if they won't hire me?" Her heart gave a sickening thump. "I'm not sure I could take any rejection at this point."

"Why wouldn't they hire you?" Steven asked. "You're smart. You're fashionable. You're beautiful. And you're my sister."

Jessica laughed, and so did he.

"I'm your biggest fan, Jessica," he said warmly, giving her hand a squeeze.

"You're my only fan," she said.

"That's not true."

Right now, Jessica felt as if it was. She felt as if she'd made a fool out of herself over and over again. Broken her heart one time too many. She was a mess and felt like the object of unwelcome curiosity and pity.

The story about Jessica and the handsome professor who'd selflessly taken his own life in an effort to protect her from an insanely jealous wife had spread across campus like wildfire. It had made Jessica reluctant to even leave her room if she didn't have to. But staying in her room just meant more time to brood and be depressed.

Steven was right. She needed something to take her mind off her troubles. School wasn't going to do it. And her sorority wasn't helping her right now. Another man was absolutely the last thing in the world she needed. So maybe a job was the way to go. She picked a pen up off the table and drew a circle around the Taylor's ad. "I'll go over there tomorrow," she said.

Billie opened the case to the old classical guitar she'd bought at the secondhand store last year. She loved Steven's sisters. And Tom Watts was smart and entertaining. But she'd been glad to see them all leave after Steven had helped Jessica compose a short, one-page resume on the computer. Billie had a guitar lesson tomorrow, and the piece she was working on was still a little rough.

Steven chattered in the background as he moved between the living room and the kitchen, finishing the cleanup. "I think being a brother is probably good training for fatherhood. I gave Jessica some really good advice—even if I do say so myself."

"Um-hmm," Billie muttered absently. She found her music and frowned over the notes of a difficult section. It was a Baroque piece. Steady, rhythmic, and complicated. Challenging her fingers and her brain.

"Jessica's always been a great kid," he went on, moving toward the desk and rifling through his papers. "She just needs a little direction. A little guidance." He opened and shut a couple of drawers, obviously trying to find a pencil or a pen.

Steven had designed and built the desk himself. It was almost as long as the wall. Not only did it have several drawers and pigeonholes, but it featured work surfaces for two people—so Billie and Steven could work together.

"Wow," he said, struggling with a drawer. "I need to sand some of these drawers. They're starting to stick. Are you having any trouble on your side?"

"Ummm," Billie mumbled, trying hard to tune him out. The dinner party had been fun, but she was ready to spend some time alone with Bach.

14

She positioned her fingers on the strings and began to pluck the first, tuneful chord.

Steven walked behind her on his way to the pencil sharpener. A series of high-pitched sawing noises completely threw off Billie's concentration.

A few moments later, Steven had returned to the desk. Billie closed her eyes and tried to begin again—but Steven started talking. . . .

"You know, when I was growing up, I hated being responsible for Jessica and Elizabeth. But now I'm glad I have them in my life. I like being a big brother." He tapped his pencil on the desk, then turned his head and frowned. "Why are you fooling around with the guitar? Don't you have economics homework?"

That did it. Billie drew her fingers across the strings, making a harsh, dissonant noise. "You're not *my* big brother," she snapped.

His eyebrows rose to his hairline. "What did I do?"

"Nothing!" she answered in a voice of mounting frustration. "But I'm trying to practice and you keep sharpening pencils and talking. And now you're treating me like one of your sisters—telling me what my priorities should be."

Steven's lips curved inward, like a man trying hard not to lose his temper. "Okay," he said finally, in an elaborately patient voice. "I'm sorry. But if I remember correctly, *you* asked *me* to make some time for you tonight because you needed help with your economics homework. And since economics is your major and music is your hobby, it just seems to me that the appropriate use of your time and mine is getting the economics homework done."

Billie's heart sank, and she felt a stab of guilt. "I did ask you for help. You're right. I'm sorry I snapped." She put the guitar in the case and shut it regretfully.

Bach would have to wait. Steven and her economics homework came first.

Tom and Elizabeth sat on a bench in front of Dickenson Hall, where Elizabeth and Jessica shared a room. After dinner Tom had driven both girls back to the dorm.

Jessica had gone upstairs immediately, but Elizabeth had remained downstairs to have a few private moments with Tom. His arms were around her waist and his lips traveled from her mouth to her neck. "Mmmm," he murmured into her neck. "It's nice to finally have some time together. It feels like months since we've been alone."

Elizabeth smiled and began to gently wriggle out of his embrace. "I hate to say this, but . . ."

"You have to be with Jessica," he finished for her in a slightly injured tone.

Elizabeth said nothing, letting him jump to the logical conclusion. It seemed like Jessica was always recovering from some major trauma. And Elizabeth was always leaving Tom to be with her.

Tom was usually a good sport about it. He was sensitive, understanding, and very fond of Jessica.

But he was also human. And Elizabeth knew it was hard on him to have so little of her attention.

This time, though, her reasons for leaving had nothing to do with Jessica. But she couldn't tell him that. Elizabeth hated to lie. And she hated blaming something on Jessica that wasn't her fault. But she couldn't tell Tom where she was really going.

While she was still searching for an excuse, Tom sighed and reluctantly released her. "It's okay," he said, standing up to walk her to the front door of the dorm. "You do what you have to do."

Elizabeth threaded her arm through his as they walked through the soft evening breeze, happy that she didn't have to make up some excuse. This way, she hadn't lied to Tom.

But she hadn't told him the truth, either.

# Chapter Two

Lila Fowler walked slowly across the campus on her way to Dickenson Hall. The cool, clear evening was lit by the full moon and stars. "I bet Jessica could use some company. Someone to cheer her up and take her mind off losing Louis."

Of all Jessica's friends, Lila knew she was the only one who truly understood how much pain Jessica was feeling—because Lila had been through the same thing.

During a trip to Italy the summer after she'd graduated from high school, Lila had met and married a handsome and wealthy Italian, Count Tisiano di Mondicci. Their marriage had been passionate and happy. But brief. Because Tisiano had died shortly after their marriage in a Jet-Ski accident.

"I hope Jessica's not asleep," Lila said out loud to no one in particular. It was fairly late, but she knew Jessica would probably still be up. The two girls had been best friends since the sixth grade, and they were both night owls.

Lila stopped and adjusted the ankle strap of the platform sandals she wore with a gauzy, forties-style bias-cut dress in an old-fashioned rose chintz print. When the strap was tight enough around her slim ankle, Lila ran quickly up the steps of the dorm and hurried to the elevator that would take her to Jessica's room on the second floor.

There was a light on beneath the door, so she knew somebody was up. Lila knocked softly.

The door opened, and Elizabeth peered out. "Lila!" she said with a smile. "Come in."

"Is Jessica here?" Lila asked, walking into the room.

"She's in the bathroom. She'll be back in a minute. Have a seat."

Lila sat down on Jessica's red, blue, and yellow quilt and leaned back against the pillows. "What's up?" she asked Elizabeth.

"We just got back from Steven's," Elizabeth said, pulling a gray sweatshirt on over her blue T-shirt.

For the thirty-thousandth time in her life, Lila wondered why Elizabeth Wakefield didn't make more out of her gorgeous body and face. Elizabeth seemed to have very little interest in clothes. Sure, she always looked nice at dances and on special occasions. But aside from that, it seemed to Lila that Elizabeth lived in straight-leg jeans, boots or sneakers, and a sweatshirt. During the day, if the sun was out, she invariably wore a baseball cap.

"Are you going out?" she asked Elizabeth politely.

"I'm meeting a friend," Elizabeth said. "I'm just waiting for her to call and tell me where."

The door opened, and Jessica walked in. Unlike Elizabeth, Jessica had taken care with her outfit. She wore pewter-colored cigarette pants and a matching short sweater that just barely cleared the waistband. Pewter grosgrain mules completed the ensemble, and the outfit met with Lila's unqualified approval. "You look great," she said.

Jessica smiled. "Thanks. I've been cheering myself up lately by shopping. Which is why I'm broke now. Fortunately, it's only temporary. I'm going to Taylor's tomorrow to apply for a job."

Lila sat up, shocked. "Taylor's. Gross. Nobody who's anybody shops there anymore. Why would you want to work there?"

"Because they're looking for sales help," Jessica answered. "And I need something to take my mind off Louis." She walked to the window, looked out, and shut the blinds with a rattling snap. Then she came back over to the bed.

Lila took Jessica's hand and squeezed it. "I know it's hard to believe, Jessica, but there is life after love," she said softly. "Trust me. I know."

Jessica gently withdrew her hand, and Lila

understood why. She'd been told the same thing when Tisiano had died. But she hadn't wanted to hear it either.

The heartache was intense. But when the happiness was gone and all you had left to remember someone by was the pain, you kept the pain—because it was better than having nothing at all.

"I like Taylor's," Elizabeth said, taking a pad and pencil from her desk and loading up her backpack.

*You would,* Lila couldn't help thinking.

"They've had lots of bargains lately. Tons of stuff on sale," Elizabeth continued.

"They've always had a nice shoe department," Lila said, determined now to find something good to say about Taylor's. Why make Jessica feel worse?

"Enough," Jessica said, giving her a cynical smile. "I know Taylor's isn't the last word in fashion. But it's a good place to start. Steven helped me put together a resume, and I'm actually getting psyched. Like it or not, I've got to start thinking about my future."

Lila shrugged. "Why bother thinking about the future since you can't predict it or control it?"

Elizabeth laughed. "That's one way of looking at it. But those of us who don't have multimillion-dollar trust funds have to think about the future. And plan for it. We don't have a choice."

Lila felt her cheeks flame. Why did everybody think they had the right to patronize her just because she was richer than they were? She bit back a retort, determined not to get into an argument with either Elizabeth or Jessica.

The phone rang, and Elizabeth picked it up before the second ring. "Elizabeth Wakefield," she said in a very businesslike voice. "Yes. Yes. Okay. The Canteen. I'll see you there in fifteen minutes." Elizabeth put down the phone and grinned. "See you guys later."

Elizabeth hoisted her backpack over her shoulder and left the room. Even in jeans and a sweatshirt she radiated an aura of confidence and authority.

And Jessica, for all her unhappiness, was taking her life into her own hands, trying to change the course of it. Maybe Lila was the one who had the wrong slant on this future stuff.

"Help me decide what to wear tomorrow," Jessica suggested. She walked over to the closet and began pulling out some of the new outfits she'd purchased.

Lila languidly lay back against the headrest. But the relaxed position was just a pose. She wasn't resting easily. She was feeling increasingly agitated.

Her boyfriend, Bruce Patman, was at a Sigma meeting planning a construction project.

Elizabeth clearly had places to go and people to see.

Jessica was busily making plans to get on with her life.

23

And Lila was lying here watching.

Was everybody finding a direction in life except her?

Elizabeth entered the noisy coffee bar and looked around. The place was full of college students hanging out after a night of hitting the books.

As usual, somebody was playing golden oldies on the jukebox, and the dark nightspot smelled like rich freshly ground coffee and pastries.

Elizabeth hoped she wouldn't run into anybody from WSVU, the campus television station where she and Tom worked. He was the anchor and general manager. If a fellow reporter noticed her, it would be natural for him or her to mention to Tom that they'd seen Elizabeth here.

*And* it would only be natural for them to ask her what she was doing here by herself.

Amy Briar had asked for a confidential meeting with Elizabeth. She'd made Elizabeth promise not to use her name or face in connection with any story she might broadcast as a result of this meeting.

Elizabeth had promised. And she didn't want any other "busybody" reporters spooking Amy and scaring her off before Amy could tell her what kind of scandal she'd discovered.

"Are you Elizabeth?"

Elizabeth turned and saw a very pretty, slightly built girl giving her an uncertain smile.

"I'm Elizabeth Wakefield," Elizabeth said in her friendliest voice. If this was Amy, she was nervous, and Elizabeth wanted to put her at ease as soon as possible. She nodded at a booth in the far corner of the coffee bar. "Why don't we go over there and talk. It's private and nobody can overhear us."

Amy followed Elizabeth to the back booth.

A student waiter came over, took their order for two coffees, and then disappeared.

Elizabeth smiled and waited for Amy to say something. Amy's eyes darted left and right. Even though it was dark, Elizabeth could tell that she was blushing.

"Anything you tell me is confidential," Elizabeth reassured her. "You said over the phone that you had a problem. I'd like to help you if I can. But I need to know what the problem is before I can do anything."

Amy leaned forward, and her blue eyes turned angry. "The problem is that—"

"Two coffees," a pleasant voice interrupted, placing two steaming mugs down on the highly polished wooden surface of the table.

Amy broke off immediately and waited for the waiter to withdraw. Then she leaned forward again. "Look at me," Amy said. "And tell me what you see."

Elizabeth looked at her and shrugged. "I see a very pretty girl who looks angry and embarrassed about something."

Amy picked up her spoon and stirred her coffee. "Do you see anything about me that would make someone uncomfortable?"

"No."

"Do I look unhealthy? Do I look like I might collapse under the weight of a tray of plates?"

Elizabeth wondered what Amy was getting at. This was one of the strangest conversations she'd ever had.

"My parents are divorced. My dad is unemployed and my mom has a very modest income. I'm a junior, and I transferred to SVU this semester so I could qualify for in-state tuition. But I still have to work to afford it."

Elizabeth stirred her own coffee. "No shame in that. Lots of people work their way through school."

"Right. I've worked almost exclusively in restaurants ever since I graduated from high school. I've worked in diners. And I've worked in five-star restaurants. I also did some freelance modeling when I was in New York. Runway stuff."

She pulled a folded piece of newspaper from her purse and handed it to Elizabeth. A black circle was drawn around an ad. *"Models wanted for Kitty's Restaurant. Waitress experience a must."*

Elizabeth smiled. "Wow! Looks like you're a shoo-in."

Amy nodded. "That's what I thought, so I went for an interview. When I got there, the place was closed. None of the staff was there, and I had

26

an interview with the manager in his office. When I didn't get the job, he said I didn't meet their *physical requirements*."

"What does that mean?" Elizabeth frowned.

"He said the trays were very heavy and I probably wouldn't be able to lift them."

Elizabeth scratched her head in confusion. "If you've worked as a waitress before, then you should be used to carrying trays and stuff like that. Right?"

"That's right," Amy insisted. "I offered to prove I could lift them, but he said the restaurant couldn't take a chance on a workmen's compensation suit."

Elizabeth sat forward. "So what are you telling me? I'm confused."

"So was I—until I left his office. On the way out, I walked through the restaurant and noticed that some of the staff had come in. About five waitresses were setting up the tables. And every single one of them had at least a double-D size bust."

Elizabeth's jaw dropped. "So you think . . ."

"I don't think," Amy said. "I know I didn't get the job because they don't hire women with small busts. Elizabeth—I need a job. And maybe I'm naive, but I just don't think what happened is right. You can't discriminate against people because of their color or religion or a disability. So why is it okay to discriminate against a woman because of her bra size?"

"That's disgusting," Elizabeth said. "But I don't know what to think about it. I mean, there are times when, well, the nature of the work has certain physical requirements. If you're a model, you know you have to be a certain height. And you have to be thin and photogenic or graceful or whatever. Lots of people would love to be a model, but they don't meet those physical requirements. Are *they* being discriminated against?"

Amy took a sip of her coffee. "No," she said gloomily. "Yes," she amended. "But meeting the physical requirements goes with the territory there. And if they'd been advertising for topless dancers or something, that would be another thing. But they advertised for models and waitresses—like they were a regular restaurant. If they're in the boob business, they ought to say so."

Elizabeth chewed on her lip. This was complicated, but Amy was right. It was an interesting story, too. Now all Elizabeth had to do was prove that the restaurant was discriminating against women with less than large chests. Elizabeth and her less than large chest would have to go undercover. . . .

# Chapter Three

Billie sat in the cafeteria, scanning her economics textbook and trying to stay awake. Her economics class met in fifteen minutes. After that, she had her guitar lesson in the music department. The guitar sat on the floor beneath the table.

When she'd begun studying guitar last year, Billie had deliberately scheduled her lessons to follow her economics classes. The music lessons were her way of rewarding herself for sticking with such a tedious subject.

She rarely said much to Steven about the lessons. This morning he'd noticed that she was wearing a flowery blouse and her straight brown hair was caught back in a loose, romantic braid. He'd complimented her, and Billie had laughed inwardly.

For two years she'd been dressing up for her lessons. And Steven was just now noticing. She felt like a woman leading a double life.

Billie wondered if Steven had a side of his life that he was hiding from her. She doubted it. Steven was a very straightforward, uncomplicated man—which was what she loved about him. Whatever he was thinking or feeling, he shared it with her. And that was nice.

A hand suddenly rested on Billie's shoulder and the next thing she knew, Elizabeth was seated next to her with a cup of coffee and a pastry.

"Hi! What are you doing here?" Billie asked.

Elizabeth grinned. "I go to school here." She laughed and tore a piece off her pastry. "I have a few minutes before my next class and I needed a caffeine and sugar boost. Thanks again for last night. It was a fun dinner party."

Grateful for an excuse to close her book, Billie shut it with a snap and put it in her backpack. "Steven and I had fun too. Thanks for coming." She smiled at Elizabeth and tore a piece off Elizabeth's pastry for herself. "Oh, and Tom's a doll," she said, popping the sugary crust in her mouth.

"You're telling me," Elizabeth said happily. "Tall. Dark. Handsome. Intelligent."

"Shares all your interests," Billie said, adding to Tom's list of attributes.

Elizabeth opened a packet of creamer and poured it into her coffee. "Is kind to dogs and old people."

Billie laughed. "I hope he's got a sense of humor."

"He's got a better sense of humor than I do."

Elizabeth stirred her coffee. "I tend to get a little carried away with the 'truth and justice for all' jazz."

Billie pressed her lips together. "You and Steven both. He can't wait to get to the courtroom."

"Is corporate law about truth and justice for all?" Elizabeth asked skeptically.

"Of course." Billie smiled. Sometimes she forgot how young Elizabeth and Jessica were. The two girls thought that they were completely dissimilar, but Billie knew they were more alike than most people ever dreamed.

Both of them were action oriented. They loved people. They loved excitement. And they loved things to happen *right now*. Elizabeth was a good student and an extremely bright girl, but she was far from introverted. Jessica was having a setback right now, but when she was her usual self, she was the absolute life of the party.

Anything conventional horrified them both.

Steven was much more down-to-earth than his twin sisters. So was Billie. Steven and Billie both realized that truth and justice for all depended less on fiery five-minute television exposés than it did on someone's willingness to do the complicated, time-consuming work of sorting out tangled business and legal affairs.

When stirred on the subject, Steven could actually sound quite passionate about the importance of law and economics. When it came to business

31

plans, regulatory trends, and things like that, he became downright poetic.

But somehow, when they were apart, Billie found it hard to communicate the drama and excitement of macroeconomics the way Steven could. It was actually pretty hard for her to get excited about it herself. Steven was interested in those things, and he made them seem interesting to others—including Billie. It was largely due to Steven's influence that she'd chosen economics as a major and law as a course of graduate study.

There was a thump from beneath the table, and Elizabeth looked startled. "What's this?" She peered beneath the tabletop. "You've got a guitar!" she exclaimed.

Billie nodded. "I take lessons in the music department. It's just an elective. For fun."

"Yo, Billie!"

Billie looked up and saw Chas Brezinsky and Mickey Tomako walking in her direction. Chas carried a tray with two plates of spaghetti and two sodas. Behind him, Mickey carried his French horn in one hand and Chas's violin in the other. "May we join you?"

"Of course," Billie said. She moved her things to make room and introduced them to Elizabeth. Chas nodded hello and flipped his long brown braid off his shoulder. Mickey's dark straight hair hung loose and was combed straight back from his high forehead. They looked like they belonged in a heavy-metal band. But both were highly trained classical musicians.

"I heard the end of your lesson the other day," Chas said to Billie. "You're getting into some very tricky stuff there."

"Is that right?" Mickey gave Billie an interested look. "I'd like to hear what you're doing." He turned to Elizabeth. "There aren't too many people who are as versatile as Billie. When are you going to do a recital?" he asked, shifting his attention back to Billie.

Billie rolled her eyes. "I've told you guys a thousand times. Music is an *elective*. I'm not recital material."

The boys exchanged a look, and Mickey turned down his mouth in mock dismay. "If *she's* not recital material, what does that make us?"

"Dog food," Chas said, looking equally worried. "All I know is it took me five years to develop the amount of technique she's mastered in two."

Billie blushed, gratified by their praise. Chas and Mickey were both on full scholarships. They were considered two of the most gifted students in the music department.

When she'd first begun running into them in the music library and coming in and out of the rehearsal rooms, Billie had been totally intimidated—certain that they would despise her as an amateur. But both men had been unfailingly kind, interested, and complimentary. And it had given her the confidence she needed to tackle tougher and tougher pieces of music.

"Well, as much as I hate to walk out on compliments and handsome men . . ." Billie laughed. "I'm off to economics class."

Mickey and Chas exchanged another comical look. "Economics?" Mickey scratched his head. "Does that have something to do with money?"

Chas leaned forward. "Yeah. But we don't need to worry about that stuff because we're probably never going to have any." They laughed and waved good-bye as Billie picked up her guitar.

"I'll walk out with you," Elizabeth offered. She said good-bye to Chas and Mickey and followed Billie toward the double-glass exit doors and out onto the sunny quadrangle.

They walked several yards in silence.

Finally Elizabeth spoke. "I've known you for two years," she said. "How come you never told me you were a talented musician? Why didn't Steven ever say anything?"

Billie sighed heavily. "I know it's hard to understand, but Steven just doesn't realize that I'm . . ." How could she put this nicely? Steven liked music as much as the next person, but he didn't have an ear that could distinguish between classical execution and noodling around. And since she did a lot of her rehearsing in the practice rooms of the music building, Steven really had no idea how much time she spent on it. "Steven doesn't really understand that I play at an advanced level," she said cautiously.

"So Steven doesn't *know*?" Elizabeth asked in a voice of disbelief.

"He knows," Billie said. "But he doesn't *get it*. And that's okay. He wouldn't approve anyway. College is expensive and the guitar probably isn't the best use of my time. So I try not to draw too much attention to it."

Elizabeth's eyes bulged. "This is blowing me away. You guys live together, and you're afraid to tell him how much time you spend playing the guitar?"

Angry now, Billie stopped and put down the guitar. "Elizabeth. This is going to sound incredibly patronizing, but *you'll understand when you get older.*"

"Understand what?"

"Music is great. It's wonderful. But there's no guarantee of a career in music. I choose my battles with Steven. Why fight one I don't have to?"

"But if music is what you love, and it's what you want to do with your life . . ."

Elizabeth had no way of knowing that she was voicing all the internal arguments Billie had been having with herself for a long time now. Elizabeth wasn't telling Billie anything she hadn't told herself. And she didn't feel like hearing it again.

"I love Steven," Billie said gently. "And I want children. I want a house for those children. I want to be able to send those children to college. That means making practical choices. And I've made mine."

Elizabeth stared at her with an expression that mingled sympathy, admiration, and bewilderment.

"Like I said," Billie repeated, trying not to sound as impatient and irritable as she felt. "You'll understand when you get older—because at some point, you'll be making all those same decisions yourself." She looked at her watch. "I've got to go or I'll be late for my class."

Billie gave Elizabeth a quick peck on the cheek. "I'll see you later. And don't look so concerned. This is just life." She smiled. "And mine's not such a bad one."

Jessica adjusted the leather briefcase Steven had lent her under her arm. In it were three copies of her laser-printed resume.

She looked down at her feet, admiring the sleek red suede pumps that exactly matched her red tank dress. She'd spied them in a shop window on her way to Taylor's and bought them on the spot. They were an unusual shade of red and transformed her outfit from merely fashionable to a drop-dead, bold, high-fashion statement.

Over her shoulder Jessica carried a black leather tote in which she had her brush, hair spray, makeup, and discarded leather shoes.

Jessica paused outside Taylor's plate-glass display window and checked her reflection. No doubt about it, she looked great. She leaned forward and wiped a tiny smear of red lipstick from the corner of her mouth. Suddenly she heard a roar, and the next thing she knew, someone had rudely pinched her backside.

"What the . . ." Jessica whirled around. Her hair fell over her face, covering her eyes, but she lifted her tote anyway and blindly swung it, prepared to beat her assaulter to a pulp. It made a soft, thumping noise against her attacker's arm as he deflected the blow.

"Hold it! Hold it!" a familiar voice begged with a laugh.

Jessica raked her long blond hair from her face, and her shoulders dropped. "Mike!"

He grinned and steadied himself on the motorcycle, cutting the engine so he didn't have to shout. "How are you?" he asked. "Don't answer. You look great."

His smile was so warm, and he was staring at her with so much genuine admiration, that she couldn't stay mad. Nevertheless, she did her best to look stern. "What gives you the right to pinch me in public?"

"Doesn't being an ex-husband give me any rights at all?" he asked in a hurt tone.

"No," she said bluntly. Mike McAllery's rights over her heart and body had been terminated when their unhappy marriage had been annulled—though there had been lots of nights when she'd wondered if she'd made a mistake.

Mike was impossible, irresponsible, and dangerous. But he was also exciting and sexy. He made her feel energized when she was with him.

Or at least he used to.

Right now, Mike wasn't having his usual electric effect, and Jessica hoped that he never would again. Falling in love with Professor Louis Miles had banished any romantic illusions she'd ever had about Mike McAllery.

And even if it hadn't, the lipstick on Mike's collar would have had a dampening effect. Mike liked women. And they liked him. Jessica was glad that wasn't her problem anymore.

*So why am I feeling irritated?* she wondered.

Mike cocked his head and gave her a quizzical look. "Something wrong?" he asked. He examined his reflection in the mirror and seemed to notice the lipstick on the collar of his shirt. He fiddled with the collar and turned it so the makeup was less visible. "My mother's in town," he explained. "She's very affectionate."

"You never see your mother," she reminded him.

He grinned and shrugged. "That's my story and I'm sticking to it. So what are you doing here?"

Jessica sighed. "I'm going to Taylor's to get a job."

"No, seriously, what are you doing? Do you want a ride somewhere?"

Jessica laughed. "Seriously. I'm going into Taylor's to get a job."

Mike stared at her for a moment, as if he was trying to decide whether or not she was kidding. When it was obvious she wasn't, he threw back his head and laughed heartily.

Jessica let her mouth fall open slightly and licked her lips, giving him a dead stare. "Did I say something funny?"

"You're getting a job!" he exclaimed between guffaws. "Doing what?"

Jessica turned on her new heels and walked toward Taylor's old-fashioned double doors. She lifted her arm to push the heavy entrance door open, but Mike's arm shot out over her shoulder and opened it for her. He'd jumped off his bike and was now hurrying along at her side. "Hey! I didn't mean to hurt your feelings."

"You didn't," she answered in a clipped tone, turning her eyes away and glancing around the ground floor of the store.

"It's just that . . . well, come *on*, Jess. You've never been the hardworking type."

"Uh-huh," she answered in an abstracted tone, refusing to be drawn into an argument. She walked over to the directory just inside the front entrance of the old department store. As she ran her eyes up and down the list of departments Mike babbled some kind of lame, insincere apology in her ear.

*Perfume . . . Pet Accessories . . . Personnel.* Personnel. Aha! Third floor.

It had been a long time since she'd been to Taylor's, but she remembered that the elevators were in the back.

She turned again, and this time a couple of shoppers emerged from behind a tall counter and cast an admiring glance over her outfit. Mike winked, taking note of the attention she was receiving.

"You're more . . . how shall I say it—*ornamental*," he said with a laugh. "Why don't you devote yourself to the pursuit of pleasure like your friend what's her name . . . Lila Fowler?"

Jessica stepped into the elevator and pressed the button for the third floor. "Because I don't have a trust fund," she said as the doors began to close.

He reached out and let the door bounce open off the flat of his palm. "What if I made a fortune and gave it to you? Would you devote your life to me?"

"Never in a million years," she answered, meaning it with all her heart. She pressed the Door Close button and fluttered her fingers at him. "Bye!"

He grinned and pushed his dark hair back off his forehead. The last thing she saw before the doors shut with a clang was the sparkle in his eyes.

Once the door was safely shut, Jessica let her lips curve into a smile. Mike made her crazy. And he was hazardous to her mental health.

But when he wasn't making her feel awful, he made her feel great. And right now, that was exactly what she needed to get her into the personnel office and land that job.

# Chapter Four

"Ms. Wakefield?"

Elizabeth nodded and smiled.

"I'm Peter O'Connor, the manager. You spoke to me on the phone. Come in." He opened the door wider, and Elizabeth stepped into the manager's office at Kitty's. It was slightly cleaner and brighter than the dark restaurant—but not much.

Elizabeth's nose had wrinkled with distaste the minute she walked in. The air in the restaurant was heavy with grease and the smell of stale beer. She'd walked right through the restaurant to the back office, but she couldn't help noticing the seductive pictures of women hanging on the dark gray shingled walls. None of the women in the pictures were nude, but they wore thong bikini bottoms and minuscule tops or wet T-shirts that left nothing to the imagination.

It was still fairly early in the day, and there

weren't many lunch customers. But the few customers who *were* there appeared to be college-age men and a sprinkling of young businessmen in suits. The bar area was empty, and the rock and roll was turned down to a fairly low volume.

The waitresses were still setting up some tables, and Elizabeth noticed that they wore tight T-shirts and headbands with cat ears attached to them.

Amy was right. Every waitress had a large bust, and the low-cut T-shirts showed a lot of cleavage.

"Sit down," Mr. O'Connor invited, gesturing toward an empty chair next to his desk. She took a seat and he closed the door, shutting out the music altogether.

He sat down himself and pulled an application form from his drawer. "So . . . let me just get some basic information. How much waitressing experience have you had?"

Elizabeth removed her raincoat. When she was sure she had his attention, she squared her shoulders, thrusting her heavily padded bosom forward. "None," she said in a breathy voice. "But I'm a fast learner, and I'm really interested in the restaurant business. Will my lack of experience be a problem?"

She waited for him to put the application form back into his desk and politely tell her that they required at least some prior experience. But he just smiled and winked. "It's no problem. If you're a fast learner, you'll catch on. Now, then, let me get your social security number, address, and all the information we need for our employment files. Have you *ever* had a job before?"

"No," she answered.

Again, she was sure that her response would elicit a polite, but marked, drop in enthusiasm.

"Well," he said pleasantly. "This will be a good experience for you. You'll get a taste of the working world."

Elizabeth couldn't believe it. She'd padded her bra to a size D at least, but her arms and shoulders weren't much bigger than Amy's. "Do you think I'll be able to lift the trays?" she asked, a concerned look across her face.

"We have busboys to bring the heavy trays out," he said absently, filling out some paperwork. "Can you start tonight?" he asked. "Our head waitress, Glenda, is on duty and she's great at training the new girls."

"Sure," Elizabeth said. Her eyes rested on a calendar that hung over his desk. It was all she could do not to gasp. The calendar picture was of a naked woman wearing cat ears sprawled across a sofa.

"I won't be expected to do anything like . . . that?" she asked in a voice of alarm, pointing to the obscene photograph.

"Absolutely not," he said in an abrupt tone. "Kitty's Club Calendars are a separate merchandising venture. Kitty's Restaurant is a legitimate food establishment. We are not in the adult entertainment business, which is why we can hire waitresses under twenty-one. Our only requirement for our wait staff is that they provide professional food and beverage service to our patrons."

*Yeah, right*, Elizabeth thought. She wiggled her shoulders again, drawing attention to her huge bosom. Thanks to Amy, she was going to get a darn good story *and*, she hoped, put a stop to a system that valued women for their curves and nothing else.

"It's still a little rough. But you're improving," Mr. Guererro said kindly in his lightly accented voice.

"You're being nice," Billie said as she returned her guitar to the case. "I know I wasn't as polished as I should have been. But I just couldn't seem to find time to practice last week."

Mr. Guererro handed Billie her shawl and smiled. "You will never *find* time to practice," he said, walking her to the door. "You have to *make* time to practice."

It was a gentle rebuke, but she blushed to the roots of her brown hair. Mr. Guererro had no obligation to give lessons to non-music majors. He *made* time for her. To show up for her lesson ill prepared—and basically say that she'd had more important things to do—was not only irresponsible, it was rude. "You're right," she said immediately. "And I'm sorry. I'll *make* time to practice."

"I wouldn't bother to scold if you weren't so talented," he said, winking at her so she'd know he wasn't angry. "Good-bye. I will see you next week." He closed the door, and Billie turned away, feeling elated and ashamed at the same time.

*I wouldn't bother to scold if you weren't so talented.* Mr. Guererro was a kind and patient teacher, but he wasn't generous or lavish with praise. So when he gave her a compliment, Billie knew he meant it. It made her determined to find—*make,* she mentally corrected—the time to practice this week.

She heard a thumping piano inside one of the rehearsal rooms accompanied by a feverish violin. It wasn't a piece she recognized and she paused, listening to the fusion of classical and jazz techniques. Within seconds, she recognized Chas's playing and smiled. He was playing with Brad Lyndon.

A year ago, she couldn't have distinguished between one musician and another, but now, after two years of studying and listening outside rehearsal rooms, she was learning to recognize the different styles.

Billie listened as the violin melody built in intensity along with the crashing chords of the piano. Chas modulated up, and the piano followed. The melody increased in complexity and suddenly, the violin went squealing out of control.

The sound was so horrible, Billie's toes curled in her shoes.

The piano and violin came to a stop, and both musicians burst into hysterical laughter. She could hear Brad kidding Chas, and then they both laughed again. The door flew open, and Billie fell back in surprise.

"Eavesdroppers rarely hear anything good," Chas said with a grin.

"I heard a lot of good stuff," Billie retorted.

"What did you think of the big finish?" Brad asked with a laugh. "Wow, Chas, the last time I heard a noise that awful was when I tried to bathe my cat."

Chas laughed, and the two boys left the rehearsal room. Brad toyed with the key as they all walked in the direction of the music library, where keys to the rehearsal rooms were checked out and turned in.

"The last time I made a noise that awful was when I stripped the gears off my father's car," Chas joked.

Billie thought it was incredibly cool the way they could goof up without embarrassment. They were so good and so professional that they weren't embarrassed by their mistakes the way she was.

"I'll turn in the key," Brad said. "And I've got some stuff to listen to in the recording library, so I'll say good-bye here."

"Thanks for practicing with me," Chas said, tossing his brown braid over his shoulder.

"Anytime." Brad smiled back. "It was fun. Billie, good to see you."

Billie nodded good-bye, and she and Chas wandered out the front doors and into the sunlight. A couple of music students wearing headphones sat on the front steps of the old building.

Chas grimaced. "I've got a lot of listening to do tonight too. I've got a drop-needle test tomorrow."

"A drop-needle test?"

Chas nodded. "That's where the professor puts on a record, randomly drops the needle, plays fifteen seconds of the piece, and you have to identify the piece and the composer."

"Wow!" Billie said enviously. "That sounds a lot more interesting to study for than an economics exam."

Chas chuckled. "Almost anything sounds more interesting than studying for an economics exam."

"Oh, it's not *that* bad," Billie said, feeling now as if she needed to defend her major.

"I know. I guess it's just that music is the only thing I've ever been interested in. I can't imagine doing anything else. And it's hard for me to understand somebody like you. You have all this talent, and you don't seem to have any desire to just . . . go for it."

"I guess I'm too practical," Billie said. "There are so few guarantees in music."

"I'll say," Chas agreed. "And with synthesizers and all the sound technology that's coming out, musicians will probably be obsolete someday."

"So why . . ."

"Because I can't imagine doing anything else. And I don't care how much technology they develop. You might be able to synthesize strings for pop songs and commercials, but there will never be anything like a live symphony orchestra. Never."

"But there aren't that many symphony orchestras," Billie pointed out. "You might not get a job with one."

"But I might." He turned and looked directly at her. "I have to try. It's an obligation. You don't just say to the great beyond, 'Hey, thanks for the talent, but I think I'll take a pass.' No. If you've got it, you're expected to use it. Or at least try to use it. And as long as I'm young, healthy, and don't have any dependents, why shouldn't I devote myself, body and soul, to music?"

Billie's lips moved slightly, but she said nothing. What could she say? He was absolutely right. In his own artistic way, he was as down-to-earth and realistic as Steven.

And in his own artistic way, he was just as passionate and principled. He didn't take his talent for granted the way some rich kids took their privileges for granted.

Chas was thankful and keenly aware that he'd been singled out in a unique way. For him to turn his back on his talent, his calling, was as rude and ungrateful as her arriving for her lesson unprepared.

Billie looked up at the blue sky, feeling her entire belief system shift a few degrees. It was so unsettling, she almost took his arm to steady herself.

For the last two years, Billie had nurtured the belief that she was the hard worker and the music students were dallying in the arts, entertaining themselves and frankly, wasting their valuable college educations.

But now she was beginning to think maybe it was she who was taking the easy way out.

"You wouldn't by any chance be interested in working on a duet with me?" he asked.

Billie straightened. "Are you serious?"

"Almost never," he joked. "But I would like to work on a duet with you—if you have the time."

"I'll *make* the time," she promised, feeling incredibly flattered.

"Great. I'll copy the music and bring it over to your place tonight if it's convenient. Then maybe you can go over the guitar part with Mr. Guererro."

Billie smiled happily. "That would be great. Why don't you plan on having some dessert and coffee? And you can finally meet Steven."

"That's the end of your orientation," the lady at the podium announced. "Welcome to Taylor's."

There was scattered applause from the five new employees who had just attended a very dull orientation lecture in the employees' lounge.

Jessica still couldn't believe how easy the whole thing had turned out to be. She'd expected hours of grueling interviews, but all she'd been required to do was fill out an application and produce two forms of ID. Then she'd been hired on the spot by a very tired-looking woman who'd brought her and the other four applicants to the dingy lounge.

Jessica looked around and fought to keep her nose from wrinkling. This place needed paint— bad. New chairs, too. The metal folding chairs were rusted and the thick metallic paint was chipped.

*Taylor's must be hard up for help,* she thought, looking at the other four applicants. There were two men who looked like retirees. (One of them looked like he'd wandered in off a park bench.) There was a nice-looking, middle-aged woman who resembled Jessica's mother—though she didn't look too enthused about this place either.

Then there was a sad-looking, unfashionable teenage girl with terrible posture, bad skin, and a long curtain of thin, stringy, unwashed hair.

Jessica tapped her orientation folder against her gold bangle bracelet. Maybe she should just go back up to the personnel office and quit. This scene wasn't doing squat for her self-esteem. If anything, it was taking what was left of it and hammering it into the ground.

Lila was right. Nobody who was anybody would shop here *or* work here. Jessica was sorry she'd wasted her money on new shoes.

Jessica stood up and then froze when the door opened and a voice asked, "Is there a Jessica Wakefield in here?"

The voice belonged to a tall woman. She had

thick auburn hair that hung in waves around her shoulders, and she wore the best-looking suit Jessica had ever seen. It was black and modeled after an old-fashioned riding habit. The jacket was long and nipped in at the waist. The skirt was straight and fitted with a drape of material at the hip that suggested a bustle.

She looked like she was in her late twenties, maybe even her early thirties, and she was the most stylish thing Jessica had seen in Taylor's since she walked in.

She was also everything Jessica wanted to be when she got older. Not only was she gorgeous; she radiated an aura of complete self-possession. Her burgundy lips parted in a wide smile as she strode toward Jessica with her hand extended. "How do you do, Jessica? Welcome to Taylor's. I'm Val Tripler, and I'm supposed to take you to meet your supervisor. Ready?"

Jessica picked up her purse. Val Tripler's appearance had dispelled some of her reservations about working here. No sense in being hasty. She could always quit later if she didn't like it. "What will I be doing, Ms. Tripler?"

"Call me Val." She flashed Jessica a warm smile and gave her a long look from head to toe. "You look great."

Jessica blushed with pleasure. It was nice to finally meet someone with enough fashion sense to understand what she'd pulled together. "I think we'll start you out in Young Fashions and

Accessories. That's on the first floor next to Men's. Mr. Farley supervises that entire floor, so you'll be training under him."

"Cool!" Young Fashions sounded pretty exciting. Probably a lot of funky, cutting-edge stuff. And if Mr. Farley was anything like Val, he was probably young, good looking, fun, and into fashion.

She felt a rush of gratitude toward Steven as she followed Val down the employee stairs to the first floor. This was exactly what she needed. Being surrounded by professional, interesting people who'd appreciate her for what she had to offer.

When they exited the stairwell onto the first floor, Jessica saw two men standing at a counter examining some neckties. One was a young man with an earring, a shaved head, pressed military pants, and a sport coat with leather patches on the sleeves. It was a very fashionable look for a young guy. He was holding up the tie and discussing it with an old fat man.

"Mr. Farley," Val called out. "Excuse me for interrupting, but I want to introduce you to your new employee."

Jessica smiled at the young man and eagerly waited for him to say something welcoming, but his eyes flickered over her without interest. A look of annoyance passed over the face of the old fat man as he hurried in their direction with a scowl. "I'm very busy," he snapped. "What's her name?"

"Jessica Wakefield," Val answered, completely unperturbed at his rudeness.

Mr. Farley didn't even look at Jessica, never mind shake her hand or say something about it being nice to meet her. He waved his hand in the direction of the next department. "Show her how to use the cash register," he said curtly. "I'll be along in a bit."

With that, he rudely turned away and resumed his conversation with the young guy.

Val winked at Jessica. "Don't mind Mr. Farley. He's been here since the place opened and he's getting ready to retire. He's cranky, but if you do your job properly, you won't have any trouble."

Jessica couldn't help throwing Mr. Farley a worried glance over her shoulder. She didn't know what Val's definition of trouble was, but that Farley character looked like trouble with a capital *T*.

# Chapter Five

"Okay," Tom said, crushing his paper coffee cup and tossing it into the wastebasket. "Cut a couple of minutes off the leader and we'll be ready for tomorrow's seven A.M. broadcast."

"All right!" Greg Timmons said happily.

It had been a long session. Tom and Greg had been in the editing room for the last four hours finishing up a piece on new registration procedures.

It wasn't the stuff of which exciting journalism careers were made, but WSVU was about providing students with the news and information they needed. And they needed this information—new locations, new forms, new course catalogs, changes in course requirements, and so on.

"How about heading for Pizza Mart?" Greg suggested. "I've been thinking about pizza for the last two hours."

"I've been thinking about my *girlfriend* for the last two hours," Tom said. "If it won't hurt your feelings, I think I'll take a rain check on the pizza and see if I can catch up with Elizabeth."

"You and Elizabeth haven't had much time together lately, huh?"

"Try none." Tom laughed ruefully. He picked up his jacket, stretched, and stepped over the chairs that had been pulled close to the monitors and control panel. "You did a great job, Greg. Thanks."

"Hey! No problem. It's a good piece."

"See you tomorrow," Tom said as he left the small, hot editing room. He walked through the main office of the station, and then pushed through the exit doors.

As Tom passed the student newsstand, he ducked in to get a paper and see what the local theater listings were. *Maybe Elizabeth will be into catching a movie tonight,* he thought. He located a paper, opened it to the movie page, and picked out one or two that Elizabeth had mentioned she'd like to see.

Tom reached into his pocket, fished up a quarter to pay for his paper, and walked over to the cash register.

"One newspaper?" the clerk asked, punching the button.

"Hold it," Tom said. A bucket full of flower bouquets sat on the floor next to the counter, and he leaned down to examine them. A bunch of bright yellow daffodils and lacy green ferns caught his eye. Bright. Cheerful. Sunny. "I'll take these, too," he said, pulling the dripping bouquet from the water and handing the cashier some bills.

The clerk took the wet bouquet from Tom's grasp and efficiently wrapped it in fresh foil paper tied with a ribbon. When Tom finally left the store with the flowers and the newspaper, he felt sure he was about to earn some serious points with Elizabeth.

Once inside Dickenson Hall, Tom was lifting his fist to knock when the door flew open. Elizabeth stood there, wearing a raincoat and holding her purse. "Oh!" She blinked in surprise.

Tom blinked in surprise back. "Are you going out?"

Elizabeth looked stumped for a moment—as if she was so shocked to see him, it had blocked her ability to think.

"And why are you wearing a raincoat?" he asked. "It's not raining."

"Um, I was cold," she said quickly. "And I just heard on the radio that it's getting colder."

Tom held the flowers out toward her and smiled. "I was hoping we could go to a movie. *Two for One* and *My Sweet Love* are playing at the multiplex in half an hour."

"I wish I'd known you were coming," Elizabeth said, backing awkwardly into the room. She took the flowers and seemed slightly annoyed at having to stop and deal with them. Her eyes darted around the room until she found an empty jumbo-size soda cup on Jessica's bedside table. She plopped the flowers into the cup and smiled. "There," she said in a bright voice. "That looks great. Thanks a lot."

It wasn't exactly what Tom had in mind, but it was clear that he'd caught her by surprise. He tried not to feel hurt by Elizabeth's obvious lack of enthusiasm.

"So where are you going?" Tom asked. "Is it anything you can blow off?"

She shook her head and swallowed. "I can't, Tom. It's . . . one of my girlfriends from high school. She's having some boyfriend problems and . . . well, you know how it is?"

Tom fought a rising surge of anger. "Yeah. Unfortunately I *do* know how it is. Because this is how it is almost all the time. It seems like there's always some girl problem that's more important than spending time with me. Recently everything and everybody is more important to you than I am."

"That's not true," she argued angrily. "And I can't believe you're giving me all this nonsense."

"Do you call flowers, affection, and attention nonsense?"

"No. But I do think this *how dare you spend time with your girlfriends when you should be with me* stuff is nonsense."

Tom sucked on his lower lip, determined not to shout. "That's so unfair," he said. It was no use arguing, though. Everything he said was going to put him on the wrong side of the gender war. And he just didn't feel like playing the bad guy tonight when all he'd wanted to do was bring his girlfriend some flowers and take her to a movie. "Let's talk about this another time," he said in a low voice. "Good night."

He was almost to the elevator when he heard her running behind him. "Tom! Tom, wait!"

He turned, and she threw her arms around him. "I'm sorry. I'm really, really sorry. You've been incredibly understanding and incredibly patient, and I love you for it. I also love the flowers. And I'd love to go to the movies with you. I hope you know that if I could cancel my plans, I would." She stood on her tiptoes and pressed her lips against his.

Tom's arms circled her waist and he sighed when their long kiss was over. He never could stay angry with her for long. "The weather's supposed to be nice tomorrow. How about a picnic brunch?"

"Sounds wonderful." She smiled. "It's a date."

The elevator arrived and Tom stepped in, pushing the button for the lobby. When he reached the first floor, he realized Elizabeth had never told him who she was going to meet.

Oh, well, he was sure he didn't have anything to worry about . . . as long as she was with one of her *girl*friends.

"We're thinking about Paris for next Christmas," Lila's mom said, reaching for the tapanade and spreading a tiny bit of the black olive paste on a piece of thin toast. "What do you think? Paris or Switzerland?"

Lila straightened her short black flared organza skirt and looked around the Green Duck, the most expensive and elegant restaurant in town.

Usually Lila loved having dinner here. The dining room was the actual dining room of an English manor house that had been brought to the United States piece by piece and reconstructed by an architectural firm specializing in historical renovation.

The walls were covered with dark green silk, and the mahogany woodwork was elaborately carved and scrolled. The ceilings were high, but the room itself wasn't large and there weren't many tables.

Most people had to make reservations several days in advance, but Mr. Fowler had a table reserved for his personal use every night whenever he was in town.

The tables were covered with snowy white linen cloths, and the silverware and crystal glittered in the candlelight. Very few restaurants in either Paris or Switzerland could rival the food at the Green Duck. Still, it would be nice to get away from the routine of college. "Either one is fine with me. Can Bruce come?"

Mr. Fowler smiled and signaled to the waiter. "If you two are still dating by then," he said with a laugh that indicated he thought that was a remote possibility.

The young, handsome waiter handed them the large leather-bound menus. They all opened them, trying to choose between the various steak and seafood selections.

"Daddy," Lila admonished as the waiter withdrew courteously. "Quit acting like this is some kind of high school crush. Bruce and I are in love. It's serious. I guarantee we'll still be dating next Christmas."

Mr. and Mrs. Fowler exchanged an amused look. Then Mrs. Fowler nodded solemnly. "Of course you will." But Lila could tell her mother was just humoring her. Mrs. Fowler's eyes scanned the menu. "I think I'll start with the Caesar salad and then have the snapper."

Mr. Fowler put on his glasses, studied the page, and then removed his glasses. "I think I will too. Lila?"

"That's fine," she muttered, taking a sip of her water. Suddenly she had lost her appetite. It drove her nuts when her parents treated her like a child. She stared at the richly colored nineteenth-century landscape that hung over the fireplace while her father ordered for them all.

A second waiter put a plate of marinated mushrooms and a basket of bread on the table. "So what are you guys doing in town?" Lila asked, changing the subject in an effort to avoid an argument.

"I have some business in the area," Mr. Fowler answered, picking up the mushrooms and passing them to her. "It's going to take quite a few days to work everything out, so your mother and I are staying in the penthouse suite at the Downtowner." He smiled. "I hope we'll see a lot of you while we're here. We like making sure that everything's all right with our favorite little girl."

"Your little girl is a widow," Lila reminded her father, putting a few of the mushrooms on her plate. Honestly, no matter how many times she reminded him that she was an adult, he seemed determined to think of Lila as a perennial teenager.

Mrs. Fowler took the mushrooms from Mr. Fowler and exchanged another look with him. Her mother helped herself to mushrooms, quietly put down the plate, and sat back, as if she were psychologically withdrawing from the scene in order to let Mr. Fowler and Lila talk.

Mr. Fowler's brow clouded and he nodded. "I know that, Lila. And I'm sorry." He cleared his throat, as if he were broaching a subject he didn't enjoy. "And while we're on the subject, I've spent considerable time trying to sort out your affairs."

Lila's money had somehow gotten tied up with Tisiano's estate, and the Italian legal system was making it very difficult for her to gain access to her money.

"How much longer will it be before things are straightened out?"

"It might be quite a while," Mr. Fowler answered.

Lila dropped her fork, beginning to feel very

upset. "Daddy, you've got to do something."

"It's very complicated," her father said.

"Can't you explain it?"

"I'm afraid that unless you know something about business and international banking, you'll be hopelessly confused."

Lila's mother leaned forward. "Don't worry, darling. We'll see to it that you have plenty of money. You'll continue to get a very large allowance from us each month, just as you always have."

"I know," Lila said, trying not to sound as upset as she felt. "But it's not the same. I want to feel like a grown-up. I *am* a grown-up, and . . ."

"Of course you are," Mr. and Mrs. Fowler both said in a voice that sounded so unconvinced, it made Lila long to throw a tantrum. But she kept her temper in line.

"I guess I'm worried about my future," she said.

"I'm glad you mentioned the future," Mr. Fowler said. "Because I've been giving it a lot of thought myself."

"Really?"

"I'm getting older and as you know, my business affairs are extensive and becoming more complicated every day."

Lila sat up straighter and her heart began to beat faster. Maybe her father was planning to bring her into his business. Train her to take over his vast empire.

Mr. Fowler reached into his breast pocket and handed Lila a small folded piece of blue paper. She opened it. It was a check. A very large check. "I don't understand," she said.

"It's never too soon to start a savings account," Mr. Fowler said. "I want you to take that, put it in something safe, and start saving for your future. I might not always be around to run things, and I want to make sure you have something to fall back on in the event that I'm not able to oversee my own affairs or yours."

Lila's heart sank. So this was the way he saw her future. He would give her checks to put in a savings account and take care of her until he was too old to do it. Then he'd probably hand all her business over to some lawyer who'd treat her like a teenager too.

"What's the matter, honey? You look disappointed. It's a generous amount."

"I know that," she said. "I just hoped that maybe you'd thought about some kind of job for me."

Mr. Fowler looked stunned. So did Mrs. Fowler. They turned to each other and then, to Lila's horror, they began to laugh.

"Put the glassware on the cork-bottom trays," Glenda said. "It keeps the glasses from slipping off and it's safer." She and Elizabeth stood at the busing station, filling trays with silverware, napkins, and glasses so they could set up empty tables in the restaurant.

Elizabeth nodded and straightened her shoulders, trying to loosen the fit of the incredibly tight T-shirt that was stretched over her padded bosom. The cat ears on the headband pinched at her temples. She reached up and adjusted it, trying to make it fit more comfortably. "Wow, this thing is really pinching me."

"If the only thing pinching you is a headband, you're lucky," Glenda said wryly.

Elizabeth frowned. "The customers don't try to touch us, do they?"

Glenda rolled her eyes. "Most of them know to keep their hands to themselves. But keep an eye out for anybody who looks like he's had too much to drink. And be careful with large parties of men. They tend to encourage each other, and things have been known to get out of hand."

Elizabeth began to feel slightly alarmed. She knew she'd be stared at, and maybe even be the recipient of a few obnoxious remarks, but she never thought the customers might get physical. After all, the clientele wasn't a bunch of low-class yahoos— they were ordinary-looking men and college guys. A lot of them even had women with them. Still, Glenda had been around this place long enough to know what the potential problems were. "What do I do if there's a problem?" she asked.

"Tell the manager," Glenda said.

"And he'll make them leave?"

Glenda laughed. "No. He'll tell me to take over the table."

"That's not fair," Elizabeth said.

Glenda just rolled her eyes, as if she couldn't believe how naive Elizabeth was. "Stop me if you've heard this before, but life's not fair. A job's a job. I'm the head waitress. I get paid more than you do. And part of what I get paid to do is deal with loudmouths and obnoxious drunks. I don't like it, but it goes with the territory." She began stacking glasses and sighed. "Not like working at the Four Winds."

"You worked at the Four Winds?" Elizabeth gasped. The Four Winds had been a five-star restaurant in Los Angeles. It was mentioned in magazines all the time. It had an international clientele of wealthy socialites, businesspeople, and movie stars. It had closed a year and a half ago when the owner retired.

Glenda nodded. "Before the Four Winds, I worked at Smitty's in San Francisco. And I even worked in a Beverly Hills country club with an all-Hollywood membership."

"Wow! You've had major experience in some really nice places." Elizabeth began pulling silverware from the big plastic tub that held the clean utensils. "If you don't mind my asking, why are you working here? Why aren't you at the Green Duck or someplace like that?"

"The Green Duck didn't have any openings. But my name's on their waiting list. What I'd really like to do is get into management and work for a country club or a top-notch hotel and restau-

66

rant corporation. To do that, I need an advanced degree in restaurant and hotel management. SVU has an excellent program. There just aren't that many places around here to work where I can make any decent money. College towns tend to cater to college students, and college students are on college budgets. That means low-priced meals and even lower tips. A place like this is demeaning, but it's profitable. And the more money I make, the sooner I can get through with school and get out of here."

Glenda picked up her tray and signaled Elizabeth to pick up hers. Elizabeth hoisted it like a professional, holding it up over her shoulder.

"Do the other girls feel the same way?" Elizabeth asked as they entered the main part of the noisy restaurant.

"Lots of them do. But some get off on being ogled. Some aren't too bright and even more aren't very good waitresses. They wouldn't have gotten this job without their curves. So maybe it's good that places like this exist."

"Yeah! But if they're not good at their job, then you have to pick up the slack. Don't you feel kind of . . ."

"Resentful?"

"Yeah. I mean, don't you resent me just waltzing in here with no experience and getting a job?" They put their trays down on stands and began setting up a large table reserved for a party of sixteen.

"I don't resent anybody who's willing to work hard and do their job," Glenda said. "And so far, you're doing great."

"Excuse me, miss. Could we have some menus?"

Elizabeth turned and smiled at the table behind her. "Certainly," she said. She handed menus to the four young men at the table. They all opened them dutifully, but Elizabeth couldn't help noticing that their eyes weren't looking at the menus in front of them. They were glued to her chest.

In spite of herself, Elizabeth felt her eyebrows rising contemptuously. The young man who'd called her over noticed the look and flushed. He immediately turned his gaze back to the menu. "I'll have the individual busty pizza," he said, his voice cracking slightly. "I mean . . . uh, the *crusty* pizza," he sputtered in embarrassed confusion.

The other three boys covered their faces as if they couldn't believe how uncool he was. Elizabeth made no comment but simply noted the order on her pad. "That's one *crusty* pizza. What will the rest of you have?"

The other guys placed their orders politely. And they looked so embarrassed that when Elizabeth turned toward the kitchen to hand in the order, she felt a renewed confidence. If all the customers were this easy to keep in line, she wouldn't have any problems.

Still, she couldn't help feeling mildly threatened

by the obvious interest that every customer seemed to be taking in her chest as she walked through the crowded main dining room toward the kitchen door. *Good grief!* she thought, entering the kitchen. She'd never had any idea what it was like to receive so much obvious sexual attention.

Yuck! How did girls with big bosoms stand this day in and day out? She looked at the other girls, hurrying in and out of the kitchen. Most of them simply looked busy as they turned in their orders and stocked their trays. Maybe they got used to it after a while and stopped noticing.

"What's it gonna be, gorgeous?"

Big Philly, the three-hundred-pound chef, called all the girls gorgeous. He said he had a hard enough time remembering the orders, and he couldn't remember their names, too. "Four individual busty pizzas . . . I mean *crusty* pizzas," she finally blurted, turning and hurrying from the kitchen in embarrassment.

# Chapter Six

Steven sat on the sofa with Billie cuddled in the crook of his arm. Her feet were tucked up underneath her and she was busily reading some demographic and financial charts.

Over her head Steven held his own book, trying to memorize the passages of text he'd highlighted with the yellow felt-tip marker. Somehow, with Billie in his arms, studying was fifty times easier. He felt so peaceful, relaxed, and confident that the information just seemed to seep into his brain like water into a sponge.

The doorbell rang, and Steven groaned. Billie had said some friend of hers was coming by. Somebody from the music department or something. Steven really didn't feel like putting his book away, but she'd made it clear she wanted him to make her friend feel welcome.

"I'll get the door," he offered as Billie padded

around the apartment barefooted, picking up the scattered books and papers. He opened the door, expecting to see some forlorn, washed-out girl with a violin case.

Instead, he was staring into the deep blue eyes of a guy who was at least three inches taller than he was. A guy with broad shoulders, a great build, and a silky brown braid that hung practically to the middle of his back.

He wore faded blue jeans, a soft chambray shirt, a leather belt with a silver buckle, and black boots. Steven couldn't help glancing down to see if the boots had a heel that would explain the guy's height. They didn't.

Normally Steven didn't spend much time worrying about his wardrobe or his looks, but he wished he was wearing something other than an old T-shirt and the running shorts that made his legs look skinny and his shoulders look narrow.

The tall, broad-shouldered Adonis smiled. "Hi, you must be Steven."

Steven couldn't help noticing that this guy's voice was deeper than his own.

He cleared his throat and dropped his own voice to its lowest register. "That's right." But he still felt like a ninety-pound weakling talking to Mr. Universe.

Before he could say a word, Billie had ducked under his arm. "Come in, come in," she chirped. "Steven, this is Chas Brezinsky. He's a violin major—the best in the department."

"Only because I slammed Ben Kenny's fingers in the door of the rehearsal room," Chas joked. "I hated to do it, but it's a dog-eat-dog business."

Billie roared, and Chas laughed a deep, resonant laugh.

Steven just smiled politely. It wasn't really his kind of joke.

"When's Ben coming back from Europe?" Billie asked, walking into the kitchen with Chas trailing behind her. They disappeared without a backward look at Steven. He stood rooted by the door in the living room, their voices floating toward him from the kitchen.

"Mickey says he'll be back next month," Chas was saying. "And he'll be ready to start playing again. Wow! Did you make this? It looks great."

Steven knew he was referring to the half-full pan of lemon-vanilla crunch that sat on the counter beside the sink. Billie had taken it out of the freezer an hour ago so that it could defrost.

"I made it from scratch," she said in a voice that sounded pleased all out of proportion to the compliment.

Steven stood alone in the living room, feeling like a man who'd been handed a book with about six chapters missing. He'd never heard the name Chas Brezinsky until tonight, and from the way he and Billie were laughing, talking, teasing, and insulting each other in the kitchen, they sounded like they'd been best friends for years.

Furthermore, the minute Chas had walked in,

Billie had perked up like a dried-out plant after a good watering.

He could hear her chattering in the kitchen. She sounded more animated than she had in months. "Steven!" she called out. "Do you want coffee or tea?"

"Neither," he responded, walking into the kitchen to join them.

Billie stood at the counter, serving the leftover lemon-vanilla crunch into bowls. Chas stood next to her, talking away about some girl's recital and how well it had gone.

It seemed to Steven that Chas was standing awfully close to Billie. So close, that when Billie looked up to smile at something he'd said, her face was directly under his. Two more inches and they'd be kissing.

"So you're a violinist?" Steven asked, a skeptical note in his voice.

Chas took his plate from Billie and smiled at Steven. "That's right." He leaned against the counter and put a bite of the dessert into his mouth.

"So what are you going to do for a living?"

Billie dropped the knife with a clatter. "Steven!"

Chas threw back his head and laughed, completely unruffled. "There's a question you need to get used to," he said to Billie.

"Actually, I don't," she said in a firm tone, filling two more bowls with the dessert. "I'm going to law school."

74

Chas nodded and grinned at Steven. "You're not really going to let her waste her talents on law school, are you?"

Steven bit back the angry answer that was on the tip of his tongue. This guy was a typical artist type. All he knew about law or business was what he saw on sophomoric TV shows. Steven wasn't about to give this loser a chance to deliver some smug little sermon about the importance of music—so he just smiled. "Billie makes her own decisions," Steven said in as neutral a voice as possible. He made a point of looking at the clock. "Listen, if you guys don't mind, I'm going to leave you two in here and go study. I've got a test tomorrow."

Steven left the kitchen, grabbed his textbook off the coffee table in the living room, went into the bedroom, and slammed the door. He threw himself on the bed, fuming.

Three minutes later he heard the front door close. Twenty seconds later the door to the bedroom flew open. "Well, thanks a *lot!*" Billie snarled. "I've never been so embarrassed in my life. You came off like a total idiot. Do you know what you made me look like?"

Steven closed his book with a snap and rolled off the bed, glad she was giving him a chance to sound off. "I hope I made you look like a woman who's smart enough not to buy into a fantasy. I hope I made you look like a woman with a boyfriend who's smart enough not to waste his college education fooling around with a fiddle!" he bellowed.

Billie let out a disgusted snort. "What gives you the right to decide what's a waste of time and what's not? Maybe going to law school isn't the greatest career move of all time. Ever think of that? Ever read the paper, Steven? The legal business is glutted. Lawyers are out of work all over the country."

"I won't be one of them," Steven said between gritted teeth.

"Well, that's exactly the way Chas feels," Billie said. "And if you want to know the truth, that's the way I feel too."

Steven opened his mouth in surprise. "What does that mean?"

"It means I'm changing my major to music," she announced angrily.

Steven dropped the book on the bed. "Oh, great," he said in a sarcastic tone. "That's wonderful, Billie. An extremely practical decision. You know, Fortune 500 companies are just busting down the doors of the music department, looking for guitar players." He shook his head. *What's gotten into her?*

Billie paced back and forth. "Steven," she said in a shaking voice. "I know you don't realize it, but I'm considered to be very talented."

Steven rubbed his head, which was beginning to pound. "I know you're talented. You have talents in a lot of areas. I've always known that."

76

"No. I mean, with the guitar I'm *really* talented. When I play the guitar, I feel like that's what I was meant to do."

Steven felt like groaning. "Billie, music is wonderful. Man does not live by bread alone. Music hath charms to soothe the savage beast. All that stuff is absolutely true. No argument. But can we keep this conversation about the real world for a minute and consider this question—how are you going to survive in the real world with a degree in music?"

"I don't know. Maybe it's like religion. You just have to go on faith. As long as I'm young, healthy, and don't have any ties or dependents, why shouldn't I devote myself, body and soul, to music?" she blurted in a rush.

Steven felt as if she'd just thrown a bucket of cold water on him. He fell back and sat down on the bed. Had he been living in a dream world for the last two years or what?

"Steven?" she said, almost fearfully. "Say something."

He glanced up, searching her face for a clue. Had she really changed her mind about everything they'd planned overnight? "I thought we were going to get married," he said softly. "And what about children? If I'm understanding you correctly, you're telling me that your goals are changing. And if so . . ." He trailed off, not knowing what to say.

Billie's face paled. "I do want marriage. I do want children," she said.

"So how does music fit in?" he asked, genuinely confused. "If a husband and children are a tie and dependents, what . . . how . . . I just don't get it."

Billie seemed to deflate before his very eyes. Her head bowed and she pressed her fingers to her eyes. "I'm just upset," she said softly. "I don't know what I'm saying."

Steven got up and walked over to where she stood. He put his hands on her shoulders and looked at her face in the mirror. Before, she'd looked angry. Now she simply looked unhappy, and it made him feel awful.

"This is my fault," he said, turning her around to face him. "I was rude to your friend because . . ." He laughed. "I was jealous. He's good looking, and you two seemed so close. Too close for my comfort, I guess."

Billie buried her face in the neck of his T-shirt. "Chas is just a friend. I love you."

"And I love you. And I want to support your interests. The guitar is a great hobby. I'm not asking you to give it up. I just want you to be practical about the future."

She sighed unhappily. "Will you help me with my economics homework?"

"Of course," he whispered.

"Would you do it for me?" she asked in a smaller voice.

He laughed. "Well, okay. But just this once."

*     *     *

The music was four times louder now than it had been at the beginning of her shift. And Kitty's was totally packed.

Elizabeth's feet were killing her. The headband was giving her an excruciating pain behind her temples. And the tight, padded push-up bra was pressing her chest so hard, she felt like she had a two-hundred-pound man sitting on her chest.

Thank goodness she only had another few minutes before she could go home. She leaned over to clear the plates and glasses from a table and froze at the horrifying sight of a familiar face at the door. Mike McAllery was chatting with one of the waitresses.

His eyes flickered over the room, and Elizabeth sucked in her breath and whirled around, keeping her back to the door.

"Elizabeth. Could you check on table seven for me?" Glenda asked, hurrying past with a heavy tray full of drinks.

Unfortunately, table seven was near the door. Elizabeth began scrootching toward it, trying hard to keep her back to the wall and her profile from being spotted.

She made her way through the restaurant, moving sideways like a crab. "Everything okay over here?" she asked, looking at the customers at table seven out of the corner of her eye so she wouldn't have to turn her face toward the door.

"Elizabeth!" an all-too-familiar voice called out.

She felt like groaning. Somehow Mike had circled the room, and now he was looking straight at her. Or more accurately, straight at her chest. "What in the world . . ."

"It's for a story," she hissed. "Please don't say anything."

He chuckled and shook his head. "I won't say a word, as long as you promise not to tell Jessica you saw me here."

"Since when do you care what Jessica thinks?" Elizabeth couldn't help asking. She had mixed feelings about Mike. He was definitely one of those people with two sides—one charming and compelling. The other dark and destructive.

"Believe it or not, I do care about Jessica," he said. He grinned. "But don't tell her that, either."

"So then he gives me this," Lila said in an angry voice. She threw a piece of blue paper on Bruce's bed and continued her angry, restless pacing. "Can you believe my own father could be so incredibly insulting?"

Bruce picked up the blue paper, opened it, and whistled. It was a check made out to Lila and drawn on Mr. Fowler's account. "I wish I could get *my* dad to insult me like this," Bruce said.

He didn't quite get what was making Lila so mad. She'd stormed over to Sigma house after having dinner with her parents, thundered up the steps to his room, and hammered on the door.

As soon as Bruce had opened it she'd begun

ranting and raving about how they were determined to make sure she never grew up.

Lila threw herself down in the wing chair by the window and glared at Bruce. "Well! Aren't you going to say something?"

He handed her the check. "Yeah. If I were you, I'd get that in the bank first thing in the morning. Let it start earning interest."

"You sound like my dad."

Bruce shrugged. "Your dad's a smart businessman. What's so bad about that?"

"Nothing. But I wish he'd quit treating me like his spoiled little girl and think about my future." She got up, walked over to the bed, plopped down in her puffy dinner dress, and propped her high-heeled shoes up on the footboard. "What am I supposed to do with my life?"

"You mean besides spend it with me?"

She nodded.

Bruce sighed and put his arm around her. "What makes you so worried about the future all of a sudden?"

"Everybody's getting a job," she said.

"Who's everybody?"

"Jessica," she answered.

Ahhhh. Now Bruce began to see the light. Lila and Jessica had been best friends since grammar school. But they were fiercely competitive. Whatever one did, the other felt compelled to do also.

For whatever reason, Jessica was getting career

oriented, and it was making Lila think in that direction too. "What's Jessica doing?"

"I talked to her last night. She's selling clothes and accessories at Taylor's Department Store." She crossed her arms over her chest. "She said Taylor's is still hiring. Maybe I should apply for a job there too."

Alarm bells began to ring in the recesses of Bruce's brain. Lila Fowler was gorgeous, charming, rich, and smart—but she was also spoiled, short tempered, and had never done anything in her life that didn't suit her—then again, neither had he. Being a salesclerk just wouldn't work for Lila. "I don't think that's a great idea," he said.

She sat up, her face unyielding. "I think maybe it is," she argued. "If I got a job at Taylor's, I'd get to work with Jessica—which would be fun for both of us."

*Yeah, right,* Bruce mentally commented. Two hours and they'd both be fired.

"And if I got a job, it might make my dad take me seriously."

"Lila," Bruce said, taking her hand and pulling her back against his shoulder. "I think this is a really, really bad idea."

"Why?"

Bruce hesitated. He hated to tell her the truth—but Lila and a job seemed like a recipe for disaster. He didn't want her already sensitive ego taking any more blows. As her boyfriend, protector, and most ardent admirer, he had an absolute

82

obligation to keep her from walking into a situation that would knock her on her butt and keep her down in the dumps for weeks. "You're used to calling the shots," he said. "I don't think you'd be happy taking orders from somebody else or doing things somebody else's way."

"Who says I won't be calling the shots?" Lila said. "If I work hard and do well, they'll probably make me a manager or something. After all, look at my dad. You said yourself he's a good businessman. It probably runs in the family. I'll bet they make me a manager in no time. And if I like it, maybe I'll buy the store."

Bruce sat back with a sinking feeling in his stomach. There were times when trying to stop Lila Fowler from doing something was like trying to stop a freight train.

And this was definitely one of those times.

# Chapter Seven

"Wake up, sleepyhead!" Tom said in a hearty voice.

Elizabeth didn't answer on her end of the phone. She just groaned slightly.

"We have a date for a picnic," he reminded her. "How soon can you be ready?"

Elizabeth groaned again.

"Unfortunately, it's raining. But let's get some muffins and tea and have our picnic in the lobby of the fine arts building. They have some new paintings up. Landscapes. We can pretend we're outside."

"Tom," Elizabeth began.

Tom's pulse quickened. Somehow he knew from her tone of voice that she was about to back out.

"I'd love to go on a picnic, but I'm so tired. I really need to sleep for another hour."

"Okay," he said, trying to keep his voice from sounding disappointed or angry. "Go back to sleep and I'll come by and get you in an hour and a half."

There was a long pause.

"Elizabeth?"

"Tom, if you don't mind, I'd really rather do it another day. I ache from head to toe."

Now he was worried rather than angry. "Why? What's the matter? Do you have a fever?"

"I'm not sick," she assured him.

"But if you're aching, you must be sick," he insisted. "Throw on some clothes and let's go over to the health center."

"I don't want to go to the health center," she snapped. "I'm just tired, that's all."

Tom was so surprised at the sharpness of her voice that he actually turned his head away from the phone and shook it. "Did I say something wrong?" he asked after collecting his wits.

"No," she replied in a frustrated voice. "But you're just not listening to me. I'm tired. I don't want to go on a picnic. And I don't want to go to the health center."

"Fine," Tom said shortly. "Go back to bed and call me when you feel like getting together— maybe next year sometime." He slammed down the phone and angrily kicked the garbage can under the desk.

What was with Elizabeth? *She hasn't had any time for me recently and she seems to resent my wanting to be with her.*

\*          \*          \*

Elizabeth sat at her desk and chewed a fingernail. What was the matter with her? Why had she gotten so angry with Tom?

Because she was annoyed at the men who patronized Kitty's. That's why.

And since Tom had no idea that she was working at Kitty's, he had no way of knowing that her aching feet and arms were due to working a six-hour waitress shift and not the flu. If *he'd* told *her* that he ached, she would've insisted that he see a doctor too.

She snatched up the phone and punched in his number. "I'm sorry," Elizabeth said as soon as he picked up.

"Why are you on my case all the time?" he asked in a baffled tone. "I honestly don't understand the problem."

"There isn't any problem," she assured him. "It's just that all this stuff with Jessica and Louis Miles has used up too much of my time and emotional energy. I'm behind in my schoolwork. I'm keeping late hours trying to catch up, and I feel overwhelmed."

"Okay." He sighed. "I know you're overwhelmed. I just miss you. I want to be with you."

"I want to be with you too," she said. "And I'll call you tonight after I've slept and caught up a little on my homework."

She hung up the phone and chewed guiltily on her cuticle. Blaming her unavailability on Jessica was getting to be a bad habit. And so was lying.

But if she told Tom what she was doing, he'd tell her not to.

Or worse—he'd laugh and act as if it wasn't important.

And she was beginning to realize that it was important. Very important.

She stumbled back to her bed, fell across it, and groaned. Waitressing was hard work. Her feet really were killing her.

And that was no lie.

Tom pushed the hood of his rain slicker back off his head and entered the cafeteria. Elizabeth or no Elizabeth, he still needed to eat.

Steven stood in the line, and Tom hurried over. "Hi," he said.

Steven turned, took a few seconds to focus, and then smiled. "Hey, Tom. What's up?"

"I've been trying to catch up with your sister," Tom answered. "It's getting harder and harder every day."

Steven blew out his breath. "Yeah. Well, the twins stay pretty busy."

"Thanks again for dinner the other night," Tom said. "It was fun. You and Billie make a good team."

"Next!" a cafeteria worker shouted.

Steven placed his order and so did Tom. While they waited for their eggs and toast, Tom studied Steven's face. He didn't look too happy. "Something wrong?" he asked.

Steven shook his head. "Nah. It's just that relationships are hard sometimes."

"You're telling me," Tom said, taking the plate that was being handed to him over the metal shelf. He put the plate on his tray. "Elizabeth and I seem to be drifting apart. Knowing Elizabeth as long as you have, can you spare some advice?"

Steven took his own plate and put it on his tray. "No can do, man. I was hoping you'd have some advice for me. Billie and I, we . . ."

"Don't have time for each other?" Tom finished Steven's thought.

"Well, it's more complicated than that." Steven shook his head, and they slid their trays past the cashier. They paid for their food and then headed into the cafeteria to find a table.

"It's not that we don't have time for each other," Steven continued as they took a seat next to the window. The sky was gray. Almost black. And rain was drizzling down the glass. "It's that the time we spend isn't fun, or at least not fun for Billie. And now she's doing all these other things like taking guitar lessons and making new friends and . . ." Steven trailed off. "I don't know what to do."

Tom took a bite of eggs and stared glumly out the window. Then his eyes found a bright poster hanging on the wall behind Steven. "Hey, look. There's a sock hop in the student activities hall on Saturday night," Tom said. "It's a Theta fund-raiser."

"So?"

"So I think I'll ask Elizabeth to go—in advance, so she'll have time to plan. It'll be a real date. Why don't you and Billie go? It'll be a blast."

Steven looked unenthused.

"Dances are a great way to put a little spark back in the old romance." Tom reached over the table and gave Steven a shove on the shoulder. "Come on, Steven. I'll feel stupid going if you're not there too."

Steven drained his juice glass. "Okay, okay," he said, putting down the glass. "I'll get tickets this afternoon." He picked up a fork and began attacking his eggs. "Let's talk about something else now. Sports. It's safer."

Tom laughed. He picked up his fork and attacked his own eggs, laying aside his concerns about Billie and Steven. They might be having a lovers' quarrel. But no doubt about it, they were lovers and always would be. And if they could get through difficult times, so could he and Elizabeth.

"Ms. Wakefield. You're late," Mr. Farley snapped.

"I'm sorry," Jessica said. "But it's pouring out there. It took me twenty minutes longer to get here than I thought it would."

Mr. Farley crooked his finger, indicating that he wanted her to follow him. "Rain is a fact of life, Ms. Wakefield. It is not an excuse for lateness and it will not be accepted a second time. Do I make myself clear?"

Val Tripler walked briskly through the department with a sheaf of papers in her hand and her glasses on her nose. The glasses were on a gold chain. She looked very efficient—and it was obvious that she had found a way to be at work on time in spite of the rain.

"I understand," Jessica said, feeling her cheeks flush scarlet with embarrassment. She wanted Val to think highly of her, and it was embarrassing to come off like such a kid—giving some lame excuse about being late because of rain. She vowed to be more professional from now on.

Mr. Farley came to a stop next to a rolling rack and gave Jessica a head-to-toe look. He made no remark. Since he hadn't hesitated to criticize her freely yesterday—her handwriting was sloppy, her math was poor, she hesitated too long before answering a customer's questions—Jessica concluded from his silence that he had found no fault with her appearance.

She felt slightly gratified about that. Jessica had chosen carefully from her wardrobe. She wore a lime green linen mini with a white shrunken T-shirt and a lime green linen vest. Her hair was pulled straight back in a ponytail, and giant gold hoops hung from her earlobes. The whole effect was young but polished. "These have been sitting in the basement for two months," he said in an irritated voice. "I don't know how that happened or why, but since they're behind the season, we don't have any choice but to mark them down fifty percent."

"They're not out of season," Jessica argued. She took a skirt from the rack and ruffled it on the hanger to show him how light the fabric was. "In this part of California, this fabric can be worn year round."

"Ms. Wakefield, when you have an advanced degree in retail and marketing, I will be happy to defer to your judgment. But since this is only your second day on the job, and my fortieth year, I think you'd do well to let *me* make those decisions." He reached into his pocket, removed a red pen, and handed it to her. "Please cross out the price and mark each tag with the new price. Then you can put them on the sale racks."

Jessica forced herself to keep her mouth shut and when he walked away, she looked angrily around the department. If Mr. Farley knew so much, how come this store looked so crummy? The clothing on the racks looked picked over. The accessories looked cheap and didn't coordinate with any of the clothes.

Her fingers released a tag, and her hand came away with a dark smudge. There was actually dust on the tags.

She took a skirt off the hanger and grimaced. Now that she examined it closely, she could see it was a style that had been popular two years ago. She'd had a skirt like this in high school.

These clothes weren't a couple of months out of season, they were a couple of *years* out of season. Why was Taylor's stocking their store with old merchandise?

"Excuse me, miss?"

Jessica turned around and began to laugh. Isabella Ricci, Danny Wyatt, Winston Egbert, and Denise Waters were on the other side of the rack, grinning at her.

"What are you guys doing here?"

"We're here to do our Christmas shopping," Winston answered. He solemnly reached into his pocket and pulled out a piece of paper. "I know it's a little early . . ."

"Or a little late," Denise, his girlfriend, interjected.

"But we figured, why not come and give you the business and a big fat commission?" Danny finished with a wide smile. "Let's start with me. I want to buy something for Isabella."

"And I want to buy something for Denise," Winston said.

"Why don't we step over to accessories," Jessica suggested, leading the group over to a large wall of glass shelves. "We've got . . ."

"Dust," Winston commented, blowing a little gray cloud from a beaded evening bag.

Embarrassed, Jessica took it from him and put it back on the shelf. "I'm supposed to dust this afternoon. Why don't we look at scarves?" The group moved down the counter, and Jessica removed the scarf tray from beneath it and put it on the surface.

The top scarf was beautiful. Black, gold, and red with an equestrian motif.

"That's nice," Winston said. "But we're not really into horses. Do you have something with a food theme?"

"Who's this for?" Denise demanded. "You or me? I don't want anything with a food theme," she informed Jessica with a twinkle in her eye. "And neither does Isabella."

"Right," Isabella agreed. "I want something floral."

"And I want something geometric."

"Okay," Jessica said agreeably. "Let's see what else is under here." Out of the corner of her eye, she saw Val at the other side of the department. Jessica picked up the scarf to see what others were folded underneath it. To her surprise, there weren't any. All that lay underneath the scarf was layer after layer of tissue paper. "That's strange," Jessica said. "I can't believe there's only one scarf in the whole store."

"We're restocking next week," a confident voice said.

Val had appeared at Jessica's elbow, and she smiled at the group. She held a clipboard and angled it toward Jessica, as if conferring with her. "I have the order for new scarves right here. Does this look right to you, Ms. Wakefield?"

Jessica smiled gratefully. Val was just pretending to defer to her—trying to save her pride by acting as if Jessica had more authority and impor-

94

tance than she really did. "Yes, Ms. Tripler," Jessica said, playing along. "That looks excellent."

Val smiled. "Perhaps your customers could come back next week. Or they can purchase gift certificates now if they'd like." She smiled warmly at Danny and Winston.

"Absolutely," they said in unison. Danny and Winston both reached for their wallets, eager to make Jessica look good.

"How do I sell a gift certificate?" Jessica whispered in a panic.

"I'll show you," Val whispered back. She opened a drawer of the cash register and removed two envelopes. Then she summoned Danny and Winston a few feet down the counter and discreetly told them the price of the scarves and suggested an amount.

Both boys nodded eagerly and handed their money to Jessica. Under Val's watchful eye, she rang up the purchases.

Isabella and Denise made a very comic show of surprise when Danny and Winston turned and presented the green envelopes with gallant flourishes.

"Oh, Danny." Isabella giggled. "You shouldn't have."

"Winston!" Denise shrieked, throwing her arms around him as if he had just given her a diamond tennis bracelet. "*How* did you know?"

Jessica saw Mr. Farley drift across the floor past the Men's department.

"Well," Danny said, "I guess we've done enough damage for one day. Thanks a million, Jessica."

"Thank you," Jessica responded. "And thank you for shopping at Taylor's."

With much laughter and teasing, the four friends left the counter and walked to the door.

"Nice friends," Val commented.

"We will have some scarves, won't we?" Jessica asked.

Val rolled her eyes, dropping her hyper-efficient selling pose. "I hope so. For whatever reason, we've had enormous problems restocking for the last few months. And by the way, your observation about that fabric was absolutely right—but those skirts . . ."

"Are way out of style," Jessica finished.

Val nodded. "Yeah. Farley's good at the classics, but he doesn't really have an eye for what's on the cutting edge. So he probably doesn't realize that those skirts are a little passé." She trailed off and frowned thoughtfully. "What's odd is that . . ."

"What?" Jessica prompted.

"It's odd that they're even here. This isn't the most upscale store in the area," Val said. "But Taylor's has always had a certain level of quality. Lately, though, I think most of the stock is bulk purchase stuff. Odd lots. Unsold goods from other stores."

"What does that mean?" Jessica asked. She was incredibly flattered that Val was talking to her like a colleague. She was also truly interested. She'd always loved shopping. Finding out what happened on the other side of the counter was an amazing experience.

"It may be an experiment in down-market selling," Val said. "Several of the big discount merchandisers are moving into the area. There's a lot of pressure to lower the quality of merchandise and match the prices."

"If the store was doing something like that, wouldn't they tell you?" Jessica said.

Val shook her head. "Taylor's isn't a public company."

"And what's that?" Jessica asked, beginning to feel like a parrot. Clearly there was more to merchandising than just buying some stuff and reselling it.

"It means there are no stockholders. It's a family-owned business and they have no obligation to explain their decisions to anybody—especially me." She shook herself. "Oh, well. I've got to go and you've got to mark down those skirts."

Val disappeared, and Jessica replaced the empty tray of scarves in the drawer beneath the counter and locked it.

"Ms. Wakefield! I thought I *told* you to mark down those skirts."

Mr. Farley's sharp, accusatory tone set Jessica's teeth on edge and she tried not to sound as rattled as she felt. "I'm just on my way to do that," she answered. "But I had some customers."

"You're full of excuses today," he responded.

It made Jessica so angry, she felt like vaulting over the counter and knocking down his precious rack of fifty-percent-off, out-of-season merchandise.

"Never mind. Never mind," he said irritably. "I want you to show the new girl around." He snapped his fingers at someone behind him.

Jessica's eyes widened when a familiar figure stepped out from behind his back. "Lila!" she cried.

Bruce idly flipped through the CDs in the Sound Center, the local music store, wondering how Lila was doing at Taylor's. It had been a couple of hours since she'd called and eagerly told him she'd been hired on the spot.

He shoved his hands down into his pockets and walked slowly along the aisles, looking at the signs and trying to find something that seemed interesting enough to distract his thoughts from Lila.

Heavy metal. New Age. Grunge. Broadway musicals. Classic jazz. New Orleans jazz. Cool jazz. Experimental jazz. Opera. Symphony.

Bruce removed a hand and smothered a yawn. Usually he could go nuts buying CDs—accumulate an armful in under five minutes. But today—nothing.

The problem was that shopping wasn't as much fun without Lila. Nothing was as much fun without Lila.

He stared gloomily at a Best of the Rolling Stones display. He couldn't stop thinking about Lila and this job thing. If she really got into it, how much time was she going to have left for him?

It wasn't as if Bruce needed to be with her twenty-four hours a day or anything like that. They'd tried living together and realized they weren't ready for a full-time commitment.

But knowing she wasn't available to hang out, shop, or eat with him made him feel totally left out of her life. They usually spent hours every day together. And if Lila wasn't around as much, that meant Bruce was going to have to find another way to fill his time.

He couldn't think of anything he'd rather do than be with Lila, so he decided to go to Taylor's and see how things were going. Bruce hurried out of the Sound Center, turned the corner, and walked up the block. The downtown area wasn't large, and Taylor's was less than ten minutes away.

As Bruce entered the south side of the downtown area where the old department store was located, he noted that the blocks around Taylor's looked a bit seedy. And when he arrived at Taylor's, he was surprised. Across the street there used to be a bunch of nice stores and a pretty good restaurant.

Now there were a lot of cheap storefront retailers. And the restaurant had deteriorated, looking like some kind of joint. A couple of the windows were boarded over, and the paint was peeling off the front wall. He could hear a jukebox playing loudly inside. And the sign over the door said ICEHOUSE.

Bruce walked into Taylor's and spotted Lila almost immediately. She was actually waiting on a customer. He drifted closer so he could listen to her.

"Oh, no way," she was saying to a woman shopping with a teenage daughter. The daughter was trying on a purple ski jacket. "If you're going to Vail, you've got to have a better label than that. Vail isn't about skiing. It's about image. And that jacket just makes the wrong statement."

The woman and her daughter looked slightly taken aback by Lila's frank disgust for the jacket they had selected.

A man appeared behind Lila. He was obviously some kind of supervisor. "Ms. Fowler," he said in a dry tone. "May I have a word with you in private? Over there." He pointed toward the scarf department, and Bruce ducked behind a tall rack of hats so he could listen.

"What?" Lila asked in a flat, disinterested tone.

"I think one of the fundamental principles of retailing may have eluded you. We do not engage sales help to discourage our customers from purchasing the merchandise."

"They *asked* me what I thought about that jacket," Lila responded in a snippy tone. "I have to be honest, don't I? I mean, if I'm not honest, I don't have any credibility."

100

Mr. Farley cleared his throat. "If you feel that in good conscience you cannot recommend the products that we have to sell in this department, perhaps you would be happier selling something else. There's an opening in Men's Shoes."

The threat was so implicit, it was all Bruce could do not to laugh out loud. He could hear the man's footsteps as he walked away, leaving Lila to decide between devoting her sales talents to promoting Taylor's ski jackets or consigning herself to men's shoes—which was probably the retail equivalent of a bottomless pit.

Bruce stepped out from behind the rack.

When Lila saw him, she broke into a broad grin. "Bruce! What are you doing here?"

"I decided to drop by and see how you were doing."

She took his sleeve and pulled him over toward a counter. "This place is just terrible," she hissed. "You won't believe some of the stuff they have. Look at those ties."

They stepped closer so that Bruce could finger the selection of brightly colored men's ties. "I don't know," Bruce mused. "Some of these aren't so bad. I like this one." He pulled one from the rack, looped it over his collar, and arranged it under his chin. "Yeah. Not bad." He examined his reflection in the mirror.

"It's too thin." Lila giggled. "It makes you look like Charlie Chaplin."

Bruce reached for an umbrella and began

walking around the aisle like the silent film star while Lila giggled.

"Miss," the woman with the daughter Lila had abandoned called out. "Miss, I think we'll take the jacket. Could you ring it up, please?"

"In a minute," Lila said over her shoulder. She turned back to Bruce. "You know, that's actually not a bad look for you. You'd look great in some real baggy forties-style pants."

"Winston's got a pair," Bruce said, glad to have Lila's full attention.

"Yeah. You could go to that thrift store he and Denise are always talking about."

"Maybe we could go together. Tonight. When you get off work."

"Miss," the lady said, a note of impatience in her voice. "We really don't have all afternoon."

"I *said* I'll be right there," Lila snapped, rolling her eyes. She turned, and Bruce's heart thumped.

Standing right in front of her was the big fat guy who'd been giving her such a hard time. "Ms. Fowler," he said in an ominous tone. "Another word with you, please."

Bruce stepped protectively forward. "It was my fault for distracting her," he said quickly.

Mr. Farley gave him a brief and disinterested inspection. "Is this a friend of yours?" he asked Lila.

"He's my boyfriend, Mr. Farley," Lila explained.

"Would you please explain to your *boyfriend* that you, and you alone, are responsible for fulfilling your professional responsibilities. Customer service is your first priority and you know that."

Lila flushed, and Bruce felt terrible that this Farley guy was giving her so much grief—not just in front of him, but in front of the lady and her daughter and anybody else who was within earshot. "Hey! Lighten up, Farley," he said.

Mr. Farley turned an angry gaze on Bruce. "That's *Mr.* Farley to you, young man. And I am asking you to leave now."

Bruce couldn't believe how rude the guy was being. "I don't have to leave," he argued. "What do you think this place is—the Pentagon? It's a department store, pal. And I've got as much right to be in here as anybody else."

"Shall I have security ask you to leave?"

"Yeah," Bruce said, really beginning to lose his temper now. "I think you should. I want to see you do it."

A quick movement of Mr. Farley's hand brought two navy-jacketed security men from out of nowhere. "Would you show this young man out?" Mr. Farley asked.

"You can't do that," Lila protested.

Mr. Farley nodded at Lila. "Show Ms. Fowler out as well. She's dismissed as of now."

The two navy-jacketed security men galvanized into action. They were both tall, broad, and muscular. And they moved with enthusiasm—like two men who were tired of just standing around all day and looking forward to a rumble.

Each security man roughly grabbed one of Bruce's arms. He felt his feet leave the floor. "Wait a minute!" Bruce shouted. He didn't mind being politely shown to the door, but he resented being picked up like he was a ten-year-old. "Put me down."

"You let him go!" Lila shouted, flinging herself at the taller of the two as they began carrying Bruce toward the door. She jumped up on his back and wrapped her arms around his neck.

"Hey!" the guard protested. He whirled around, trying to shake Lila off his back, and in the process he yanked Bruce's arm in the opposite direction from the other guard.

"Miss Fowler!" Bruce heard the supervisor protesting.

"Lila! Bruce! Stop it," a voice sounding like Jessica Wakefield's shouted out.

Feeling like a wishbone, Bruce kicked his feet in every direction, trying to find the floor. Instead he felt his toe connect with something that felt more like a shin bone than the carpet.

"Ouch!" screamed the shorter of the two guards, letting go of Bruce's arm.

That did it. The entire first floor of the store erupted into chaos. Alarm bells rang. Clerks shouted. Security men and women rushed toward them from every direction.

Bruce wrenched himself out of the two men's combined grasp and fell heavily to the floor.

The lady with the ski jacket began screaming as

if there was a robbery in progress. Bruce jumped to his feet and looked wildly around for the exit.

Out of the corner of his eye, he glimpsed Jessica Wakefield. She was wearing something green and she was trying to pry Lila and a security guard apart. Bruce rushed to Jessica's aid, put his arms around Lila's waist, and pulled her off.

Lila's arms and legs flailed violently. "It's me," he yelled, struggling to keep from getting clipped by a flying fist or foot. "Let's get out of here before . . . oomph . . ."

He broke off as six more security people descended on them both.

"Bruce!" Lila screamed, reaching toward him as they pulled her from his arms.

"Lila!" he yelled back. He tried to lift his arms, but a huge security guy grabbed him in a bear hug and pinned his arms to his sides.

Somehow, the tangle of bodies moved toward the door amidst yells, shouts, and ringing bells. The last thing Bruce felt was a hand in the small of his back shoving him through the door.

Suddenly he was outside on the pavement. A second and a half later the door opened again, and Lila came careening out with her arms windmilling. She came to a stop when she collided with Bruce's chest.

"Ouch!" he groaned when her elbow caught him in the chest.

When he had Lila and himself steadied, Bruce looked up and saw the store's employees, security personnel, and curious customers staring at them from the other side of the doors.

The group inside backed up slightly, as if fearing Bruce and Lila were about to rush them. An intrepid security guard stepped gingerly forward and locked the door with a loud snap.

"Well!" Lila breathed, brushing herself off and wobbling a little on her heels. "I've never been treated so rudely in my whole life."

"Me neither," Bruce said, torn between amusement and outrage. "I'm not even sure what happened in there. One minute we're having a conversation, and the next we're in the middle of a riot."

Lila turned toward the door, scowled at the security guard, and then childishly blew a raspberry.

Bruce began to laugh, and so did a group of people standing across the street. He looked over and noticed that some of the IceHouse customers had spilled out on the street with their drinks.

"Come on," he said, pulling on her arm. "Let's get a cola."

"In there?" Lila asked, her brows rising. "That's the tackiest-looking place I've ever seen."

"I don't care how tacky it is—I'm thirsty. I need to chill out someplace."

They crossed the street and entered the IceHouse. Bruce looked around with interest. It was as run down on the inside as it was on the outside. But the place was packed like a beachfront bar during spring break.

The customers were upscale and hip, dressed ultra-casually. Bruce ordered a couple of sodas at the bar and wandered over to the back window. BMWs, Porsches, Jeeps, and motorcycles filled the parking lot. He went back over to the bar and paid for their sodas.

Lila straightened her disheveled hair and sighed. "What a day!"

Bruce put an arm around her. "Don't worry. It was your first job. And you lasted"—he looked at his watch and began to laugh— "a little over two hours."

"It's not funny," she said quietly.

Bruce realized she wasn't amused. "Okay," he agreed. "It's not funny. But it's not tragic, either. I mean, let's face it. It's not like you *needed* the job."

"I have a hard time believing you need this job, Ms. Wakefield," Mr. Farley said angrily. "I've never seen anyone treat their employment as casually as you do."

"But I do need this job," Jessica protested, on the verge of tears.

"This is a department store. Not a malt shop. We don't want our employees encouraging their friends to make this a hangout."

"Bruce is *Lila's* boyfriend, not mine."

"But I saw a group of young people earlier who seemed to be here expressly to see you."

"My friends did come by. But they didn't come

107

here to hang out," Jessica explained with as much dignity as she could muster. "They came to shop."

"Oh? And what did they buy?"

"Nothing, but . . ."

"I'm sorry, Ms. Wakefield. I'm going to ask you to go upstairs, pick up your paycheck, and come back when you're ready to work like an adult."

"Is there a problem here?" Val Tripler materialized behind Mr. Farley and gave Jessica an inquisitive look.

"Mr. Farley thinks my friends didn't come here to shop," Jessica said, choking on her tears.

"They certainly were shopping," Val said tartly. "But we didn't have the stock they wanted. So they bought gift certificates instead."

Mr. Farley looked slightly uncomfortable. "I didn't know that."

"Ms. Wakefield may be encouraging her friends to drop by, Mr. Farley, but isn't that a good thing? Don't we want our sales force to bring in customers if they can? You yourself have said that the nucleus of a clientele is often comprised of one's friends."

Jessica listened with admiration to Val. She was wiping the floor with Mr. Farley, but she never sounded the least bit disrespectful or argumentative. She never lost her smile or her charming tone of voice, and it was obvious that Mr. Farley was speechless.

Jessica took mental notes. This was a good

technique for diffusing antagonism, she decided—not that she'd ever have a chance to use it. It was becoming increasingly clear to her that Mr. Farley didn't like her. And it was becoming increasingly clear to her that she didn't like him or her job at Taylor's.

Mr. Farley removed his glasses and wiped them with his handkerchief. "You have a point, Ms. Tripler." He replaced his glasses and gave Jessica a hard look. "I'll overlook this incident. But if anything like it happens again, you're fired." And with that, Mr. Farley stalked away toward hosiery.

"Thanks," Jessica said, giving Val a smile. "I appreciate it, but I think you went to a lot of trouble for nothing. I'm going to wind up getting fired anyway."

"No, you won't," Val said. "Everybody's first job is tough. But you're in the right business."

"What makes you say that?"

"I can tell by looking at you. I've been around long enough to know who's got retailing in their blood."

Jessica laughed.

"I'm serious. You've got a nose for what's in. You're stylish enough yourself to be convincing as a salesperson. And you've got a lot of personality."

Jessica smiled, beginning to feel a little less discouraged about her situation.

# Chapter
# Eight

"Thanks, Isabella." Steven put his change and the tickets to the sock hop in his wallet.

"I'm really glad you're coming," Isabella said, smoothing her long black hair behind her ears. It was late afternoon, and she sat at a long table set up in the crowded hallway of the university center. Above her head hung an oversize pair of papier mâché saddle oxfords advertising the fifties theme dance. "We're hoping to get a major crowd for this event. But sometimes you upperclassmen act like you're too cool to come to campus dances."

Steven chuckled. "It's not that I think I'm too cool for dances. I'm too uncoordinated."

Denise came hurrying up the hallway with a tin box under her arm. "I got a bunch of one-dollar bills from the bursar," she said, taking a seat next to Isabella. She grinned at Steven, and he smiled back. "So you're coming to the sock hop? That's great. We were wondering if we should try to get Jessica to come. What do you think? You know, lately she's been . . ." Denise trailed off.

But she didn't have to finish—Steven knew exactly what she meant. "I think she's coming out of it. You know she's working at Taylor's now?"

"We know," Isabella and Denise answered in unison.

"We were there this morning." Denise grinned. "And Winston and Danny bought us gift certificates."

"How did things seem to be going?" he asked.

Isabella and Denise looked at each other and shrugged. "Fine," Isabella answered. Before Steven could ask any more questions, a group of students appeared at the table, eager to buy tickets to the dance.

"Later," Steven said, waving to Denise and Isabella, whose attention was now taken up with counting money and making change.

Steven wandered outside onto the quad and headed in the direction of the library. Billie usually went there after lunch and studied for an hour before her history class. He'd find her and tell her about the dance.

Last night while he'd finished Billie's economics homework for her, she'd fallen asleep. This morning they had both been in a hurry to get to campus and hadn't had time to talk about last night. Neither one of them had seemed into it.

Having a conversation with Billie about the

sock hop would be a good way to get things back to normal again. Billie liked dances and parties. She was a lot more outgoing than he was.

He turned the corner of the administration building and froze. Several yards away Steven saw Billie and Chas on the steps of the library, talking. Then Billie stood up on her tiptoes, brushed Chas on the lips, and hurried up the front walk.

Chas stood and watched her until she'd disappeared between the automatic sliding glass doors of the building.

Steven remained where he was, his heart pounding. There were fifty logical explanations for what he had just seen. Steven could imagine the conversation they must have just had.

*Billie: "Chas, I'm so sorry Steven acted like a grump last night. He's really a great guy."*

*Chas: "No problem. Don't worry. One day we'll all get together for a burger and laugh about it."*

*Billie: "Thanks, Chas."* Peck. *"See you."*

It would make perfect sense under the circumstances. And Billie was a very affectionate girl.

So why did Steven feel like breaking something?

Steven turned and strode back toward the parking lot. He'd lost interest in the dance. What he needed right now was some time alone in the apartment.

Lila marched through the lobby of the lavish hotel where her parents were staying. It was dinnertime, but she wasn't hungry. She'd had some nachos with Bruce at the IceHouse.

Just thinking about that place raised her irritation level a couple of notches. The minute they'd gotten their sodas, Bruce had disappeared into the back room to watch some people play pool and stupid video games.

For some reason, he'd been totally thrilled with the place. But to Lila, it was a dump. The floor was dirty. The glasses were plastic and cloudy. And the staff looked as gross as some of the customers.

Bruce had gotten all excited about playing pool with two tattooed guys who smoked. After what had seemed like an eternity, Lila had left by herself, driving back to campus on her own and getting madder and madder by the minute.

How dare Mr. Farley treat her like . . . like . . . like she was just anybody. She hadn't come out and told him that she was Lila Fowler, as in Fowler Enterprises, but anybody who was anybody in that part of California knew the name Fowler and should have made the connection.

Obviously Mr. Farley was so out of it, and beneath her, he didn't even *know* what the name Fowler stood for.

And if the store had *anybody* in personnel with any smarts at all, *somebody* would have noticed the name on her application form, made discreet inquiries, and immediately made her a supervisor— OVER that loser Farley.

A subservient desk clerk recognized Lila and

immediately picked up the house phone to call her parents and alert them that she was on the way up.

Lila gave him a grateful but distant smile. Now *this* was more like it.

The large, ornate elevator carried her to the penthouse suite that the hotel reserved for her parents. The door of the suite opened as she stepped off the elevator and her father beamed happily. "Lila! This is a surprise."

Lila walked past her father into the elegant living room of their suite. She noticed that her father's laptop was set up at the desk and papers were strewn all around the room. He was working—probably on some multimillion-dollar deal. "Daddy, I want you to buy me something," she announced.

"Anything, sweetheart. What do you want?"

"I want you to buy me Taylor's Department Store."

The smile abruptly left her father's face. "Why?" he asked curtly.

"Because I want to fire a certain Mr. Farley."

Mr. Fowler closed the door and gave Lila a quizzical smile. "Do I know Mr. Farley?"

"Of course not," Lila snapped. "He's a horrible little know-nothing drone in Taylor's Department Store, and he *fired* me!"

"What are you talking about?"

Briefly Lila described the scene that had taken place that afternoon.

Mr. Fowler sat for a moment in stunned silence;

then he threw back his head and roared with laughter. Lila sat up, feeling more affronted than she had that afternoon. "It's not funny!" she shouted.

Her father nodded. "Oh, yes, it is."

Lila stood. "Daddy! Don't you have any respect for me at all? How can you let somebody like that fire your own daughter?"

Mr. Fowler took her hand and pulled her back down into her seat. "I'm sorry, sweetie. But Mr. Farley, whoever he is, has my respect. He's a brave man."

"He's a stupid man!" Lila retorted. "He didn't know who I was."

"He knew exactly who you were," Mr. Fowler corrected.

"But . . ."

Mr. Fowler reached into his pocket. "Here." He removed two hundred dollars and handed it to her. "Why don't you get Bruce and go out to dinner. Forget all about Taylor's."

Lila's anger began to fade. She wasn't mad anymore; she was embarrassed. And sad. "Daddy," she said quietly. "I don't think you understand."

"You don't need a job, Lila," he said. "And you don't have any business taking a job from somebody who does need one."

"What are you saying?" she said. "That it's okay for me to spend money but not to make it?"

"No," Mr. Fowler said seriously.

"Then what *do* you mean?"

"Lila, I'm not sure you can understand right now," he said. "And even if you could, I don't have time to explain." He gestured toward his computer. "I'm trying to get ready for an early meeting tomorrow. I'm sorry I can't take you to dinner. And your mother's not here to help you either. She's out visiting a friend."

Lila stared at her father, feeling more miserable than she had in her whole life. He was actually asking her to leave. Her own father was politely telling her he had no time for her silly little problems.

"So what do you say? Is it a date?" Tom had asked Elizabeth over the phone.

"Tom. I'm really behind and I need to study."

"On a Saturday night?"

"You study on Saturday night sometimes."

"*We* study on Saturday night sometimes," he'd corrected. "So how about *we* both get crazy and go to a dance together instead of studying? Come on, Elizabeth. It's for charity."

Tom had called her two minutes before she'd left for Kitty's and hit her with the dance invitation.

Even though she'd spent most of the day in bed, Elizabeth was still exhausted and achy. The thought of going to a dance made her cringe.

When Tom had finally told her it was for charity, Elizabeth hadn't been able to think of a reasonable excuse not to go, so she'd agreed. And it had taken all her acting ability to sound excited about the idea.

Elizabeth found the broom in the maintenance closet and searched for a dustpan. There was a live band in the bar tonight, and Kitty's was packed. The pounding noise seemed to make the customers even more rowdy than usual, and there had been a lot of breakage. This was the fifth time she'd had to find the broom and pan to sweep up a broken glass or bottle.

Thank goodness for Glenda. She'd taken over at least two tables of drunks for Elizabeth and helped her out in a million ways, large and small.

For that matter, all the other women had been very helpful—Tyra, Sal, Katisha, Gilly.

"Elizabeth!" Glenda appeared behind her. "Could you possibly come in Saturday night? I just found out I'm going to be short two waitresses and it's going to be a busy night."

"Oh, no, I'm sorry," Elizabeth said, meaning it. She didn't particularly want to work Saturday night, but she felt like she owed Glenda the favor. "I've already made plans." That was the night of the sock hop, and Elizabeth knew that canceling on Tom would definitely lead to a fight.

"No problem," Glenda said, reaching over Elizabeth and grabbing a hand-held mop. "We'll manage."

Glenda disappeared, and Elizabeth hurried toward her station with the broom and dustpan and began sweeping up the broken glass near her large table—a loud party of six men who'd already paid their check and were getting ready to leave.

Elizabeth bent over to sweep the glass into the dustpan.

"Thanks, babe," one of the men said. The next thing she knew, he'd delivered a sound slap against her backside.

Elizabeth shot up and around, about to tell the loser to keep his hands to himself.

But before she could speak, the man smiled in a friendly, nonleering way and stuffed a wad of cash down into the side pocket of her tight jeans. "Have a nice night," he said in a cordial tone.

Elizabeth couldn't believe it. It was like he had no idea at all that he'd just—if you wanted to get technical about it—sexually assaulted her.

Her mouth was still hanging open when Gilly—big busted and giggly—came over and stood next to her.

"Did you see that?" Elizabeth demanded.

"I sure did," Gilly said happily. "That was Ronald Bernard. He's a regular and a big tipper. How much did you get?"

Elizabeth turned and stared at Gilly. Was she really so dense that she didn't think his behavior was offensive?

"C'mon, how much did you get?" Gilly pressed.

Elizabeth reached into her jeans and removed the wad of cash. "Fifty bucks," she said, astonished.

"Lucky you," Gilly said. Elizabeth's eyes met

Glenda's, and they exchanged a look. Suddenly Elizabeth realized what was wrong with this place—everybody acted as if it was okay to behave like sleazeballs.

But it wasn't.

Elizabeth stuffed the money in the back pocket of her tight jeans and continued clearing the table, feeling disturbed and genuinely confused.

Amy Briar had left a message on her machine today, wanting to know what was going on with the investigation, but Elizabeth hadn't called her back. Clearly there was a discrimination issue here, but Amy didn't want her name or face associated with the story. So Elizabeth really didn't know quite how she was going to prove the allegation, or how she'd turn it into a compelling piece of broadcast journalism that didn't dwell on the issue of bust size.

But there were more issues here than just discrimination. As a feminist, Elizabeth objected to this whole industry.

On the one hand, Gilly—for example—wasn't too bright. Where else could somebody like her make fifty to a hundred bucks in a night? Were the Gillys of the world supposed to forgo a good income because Elizabeth thought the place was sleazy?

On the other hand, was it a good idea for women like Gilly to forge their careers in places like this? What would happen to Gilly, and all the others like her, when they weren't young and bouncy? When their only assets began to sag?

This wasn't a business that was kind to women.

The Gillys of the world would do far better to find something—*anything*—that they could do. No matter what their figures looked like.

Elizabeth sighed heavily. Maybe she should confide in Tom. Sure, he was a man, but he was sensitive and had lots of common sense. Maybe after the sock hop they could go someplace quiet and have a long talk about the pros and cons of having a big bust.


"It was my childhood all over again," Lila wept onto Bruce's shoulder.

Bruce stroked the top of Lila's hair. She'd arrived at Sigma house in tears. At first Bruce had thought it was his fault because he'd gotten distracted by the pool table at the IceHouse. But slowly Lila had managed to gulp out an account of her meeting with Mr. Fowler.

She was calmer now, but still very upset.

"When I was a little girl, Dad was always busy. Always traveling. Always getting ready for a meeting." She sat up and reached for a box of tissues. "That's one reason I'm so spoiled. He felt so guilty, he always tried to make it up to me with money and things."

As superficial and spoiled as Lila could be sometimes, Bruce also knew that she was capable of deep emotions. But all her emotions were as overdone as the Fowler lifestyle. When she was in pain or hurt, she wept with the rage and anger of a five-year-old child. And when she was happy or excited, she danced on clouds.

"I got my first job today. I got fired. I got thrown out of a public place in front of a crowd of people. And you know what his solution was?" she demanded tearfully.

"What?" he asked quietly, reaching up to push her bangs from her forehead.

She opened her clenched palm, like a child revealing a shameful secret. Two damp, crumpled hundred-dollar bills fell to the floor.

"He thinks I'm a silly child," Lila said bitterly. "He thinks I'm too stupid and vain to do anything useful with my life."

"That's not true," Bruce insisted.

"Yes, it is," Lila argued. "He basically said my job in life is to spend money."

"Nice work if you can get it," Bruce joked.

Lila didn't smile, and he mentally kicked himself. Lila tended to have a lack of humor when it came to herself. He prepared himself for a shower of rage, but all his remark produced was a weary and unhappy sigh.

"This is serious, isn't it?" he said quietly.

She nodded. "It is. You'll never know how bad I feel about myself."

Bruce put his arms around Lila and hugged her tightly. He was getting good at this sensitive stuff. For once, he'd diagnosed Lila's problem correctly. She was having an identity crisis.

Now—if only he could figure out what to do about it.

Jessica drove to Steven's apartment building with mixed feelings. *Hang in there,* Val had advised.

She'd tried, but the rest of the afternoon had gone from bad to worse. Mr. Farley had watched Jessica's every move, and the strain of it was making her nuts.

She'd given the matter a lot of thought. Steven's suggestion that she get a job had been a good one. But this either wasn't the right time in her life, or else it wasn't the right job.

She was doomed to get fired, and she knew her ego couldn't sustain another major setback. She felt like enough of a failure already.

All things considered, quitting seemed like the best thing to do. But she wanted to talk to Steven before she did anything drastic. And whatever she did, she wanted to be sure she handled it in the most professional way possible.

Jessica parked the Jeep in the parking lot. Before she could get to the front of the building, Jessica heard male voices. She slowed cautiously and kept to the shadows.

Security in this building complex was good, but so many strange events had happened to her and to Elizabeth recently that Jessica tried to be as careful as possible.

When she got closer, though, Jessica recognized the voices. They belonged to Steven and Mike.

"I don't think Jessica's the working type," Mike was saying. His voice sounded laid back and calm, as if his opinion didn't mean much to him one way or the other.

"Work is good medicine," Steven said. "It's better than all the other ways people use to cope with their problems."

"Maybe for somebody like you," Mike said. "But not Jessica."

Steven's voice began to sound defensive. "I think I know what's best for my own sister."

Mike laughed. It was the who-cares laugh that had intrigued and maddened Jessica throughout the entire course of their turbulent marriage. "I'm her husband," he said. "Doesn't anybody care about my opinion? Believe it or not, I really do have her best interests at heart."

"Ex-husband," Steven corrected in a good-humored voice. "And I know you have her best interests at heart. But I think you're underestimating her. I think *everybody* underestimates Jessica. She's incredibly smart, and nobody ever gives her credit for that."

Jessica felt a rush of gratitude to Steven. She might be unlucky when it came to love, but she was very fortunate to have Steven for a brother. He might be too quick sometimes to judge or give advice, but he was maybe the only person in the world who really believed in her.

Steven and Val Tripler, she mentally corrected. But Val Tripler didn't know her very well.

"I know Jessica's a smart girl," Mike answered. "But she's just not real mature," Mike finished.

Jessica's heart began to thump with outrage. Look who was talking. Mike Mr. Immature McAllery. "Bet you the '57 Thunderbird she quits or gets fired."

Steven laughed. "Come on, Mike. You know I can't bet anything as extravagant as that. But if you'll come down to earth on your terms, I'd love to bet on Jessica."

Jessica peered between the trees and saw Mike scratch his cheek thoughtfully, squinting against the security light above his head. He appeared to think, then shrug. "Easy come, easy go. I'll bet the car against your services as handyman and assistant mechanic for two months. I'll be restoring a couple of classic sedans over the next few weeks, and I could use a hand."

Mike's business was restoring and selling old or vintage cars.

Steven laughed. "It's a bet," he said. He shook Mike's hand, then slapped him on the shoulder. "I've got to go upstairs. Billie's waiting."

"Later," Mike said.

It was on the tip of her tongue to call out to Steven and ask him to wait, but Jessica caught herself just in time. If she spoke now, they'd both know she'd overheard their conversation. And besides, if Billie was waiting for Steven, she didn't want to delay him. They both worked hard, and they needed their time together.

125

Jessica wondered if she'd overstayed her welcome over the past few weeks. Billie was probably feeling like she never had Steven to herself anymore.

Watching Steven enter the side door of the building, Jessica swallowed the lump that was rising in her throat. She hated to admit that Mike knew her better than Steven. She wanted desperately to quit, but now she couldn't.

Mike walked toward the front door. Jessica panicked and slipped as she tried to hide before Mike caught her listening.

Immediately he turned and spotted her. "Jessica! Where did you come from?"

"I just got here," she lied. "I wanted to see Steven. Is he around?"

"He was just here," Mike said.

"Oh, really," Jessica said, pretending surprise. She didn't sound very convincing, even to her own ears.

Mike's eyebrows lifted in an expression of skeptical amusement. "Really," he repeated. "And he just went upstairs."

"Well, if Billie's waiting, I don't want to bother him."

"Who said Billie was waiting?" he asked with a laugh. "You were listening, weren't you?"

Jessica was glad Mike couldn't see her blush in the dark.

He laughed the low, sexy laugh she knew well. "Why did I ever let you get away?" he asked, taking a step closer and reaching for her.

"You didn't let me get away," she retorted, pushing his hand away. "I escaped."

Unperturbed, he lifted his finger and made an invisible notch in the air. "Two points."

"I'm not here to score points off you, McAllery. I came to see Steven."

"You want to see Steven. Let me see if I can guess why. Could it be because"—he pretended to puzzle—"you hate your job and you want to quit?"

Again she was glad the cover of darkness hid her telltale blush. "You think you know me, but you don't."

"Jessica, I know you better than you know yourself," he said, his voice turning serious and affectionate. He stepped forward and put a finger under her chin, lifting her face. "Steven told me about you and that professor . . . I'm sorry about what happened. It must be pretty rough for you." There was no mockery in his voice. "If there's anything you need . . . anything I can do, just—"

"Mike!" a female voice interrupted. Over his shoulder Jessica saw a petite brunette in a cat suit and high-heeled boots standing in the lobby of the apartment building. The look on her face was filled with annoyance, and she put one hand impatiently on her hip. "Are you coming back in or what?"

Jessica angrily jerked her face from Mike's grasp. "You'd better go," she said shortly. "It's

127

rude to keep your company waiting."

Jessica turned and strode back to the gate with her head held high. She'd been needling him when she referred to her escape. But she had escaped in the truest sense of the word. Mike was handsome, charming, and sexy. But he was hazardous to her mental and emotional health.

The bedroom door opened, and Billie came padding out in her bare feet. She was wearing the green silk robe that Steven loved. "Have you seen my economics notebook?"

Steven turned down the volume of the radio and looked up from his side of the desk. "Nope," he lied. "When was the last time you saw it?"

"I thought it was in my backpack. Ah! There it is."

Steven turned his face back down toward his own book so she wouldn't see the fiery red color of his guilty face. He'd tried to be careful about putting things back in their proper place this afternoon when he'd conducted his search. Obviously he'd put the economics notebook in the wrong place.

Thank goodness Billie was messy by nature. Her textbooks and papers were always scattered on her side of the desk. His eyes rested on the guitar, with the music stacked neatly on top of it. That was the only neat area she maintained.

Steven rubbed his eyes, trying to seem disinterested while Billie shuffled through the papers on her desk. Would she notice anything else misplaced or out of order?

She let out a gasp of impatience, and Steven's heart stopped briefly. Had he left some clue of his afternoon activities?

He'd hated himself for stooping so low, but he'd carefully examined the mess of papers and books on her desk—replacing each item to its original place. He'd even gone through her drawers and examined piles of letters, cards, photographs, and mementos she kept bound up with a ribbon.

If Billie was in love with Chas, Steven was sure he'd find something concrete to prove it. A letter. A love poem copied onto a sheet of music paper. A pressed flower. Something.

"Darn!" she said, scanning a piece of mail.

Steven knew what it said. He'd read it this afternoon. She had a parking ticket that was two months overdue. If she didn't pay it soon, the charges were going to double. But he played dumb. "What's the matter?"

"Oh, nothing," she said absently, stuffing the notice in her pocket. She picked up her notebook and a couple of other things and walked back into the bedroom.

Steven tightened his lips. It wasn't just his imagination. Besides getting carried away with this music stuff, she was becoming more secretive every day. And he didn't know why.

Being messy was one thing. Flaking out like

she had the other night was something else completely. Was she honestly rethinking all they'd talked about—planning to become a *music* major? Billie had always been as practical and focused as he. So what was going on?

Steven hadn't found anything that afternoon to support his theory, but he couldn't shake the feeling that there might be more to Billie's personality change than a sudden love of the guitar.

Chas was a good-looking guy. Okay, he was a *great*-looking guy. He was also intelligent and supportive of Billie's music.

Steven swiveled in his desk chair and stared at the bedroom door. If he were Billie, he'd probably be in love with Chas Brezinsky too.

# Chapter Nine

Tom turned the page of his textbook and reached for his highlighter pen. The only good thing about Elizabeth's unavailability was that it was giving him time to catch up on some studying.

It had been two days since he'd asked Elizabeth to the sock hop tonight. Even getting her to agree to that had been something of a challenge. She was tired. She was busy. Her feet were too achy for dancing.

Finally he'd played his last card, reminding her that the proceeds from the dance were going to charity. He couldn't believe he'd actually stooped to *guilting* his girlfriend into going to a dance with him.

The door opened, and Danny came bounding in. "Come on. Your campus needs you."

"What?"

"The Thetas are responsible for decorating the

university center for the sock hop, and they need every pair of hands they can find. Come on. Let's go hang some crepe paper."

"I'm kind of busy here," Tom hedged. He liked Isabella, Denise, and the other Thetas, but he wasn't in the mood to be around all those mega-cheerful girls.

Danny came over and closed the book. "It'll only take an hour. And I promised Isabella I'd dig up some manpower. Don't make me look bad, man."

Tom sighed. "Okay, okay. I guess what goes around, comes around. I had to guilt Elizabeth into going to the dance. And now you're guilting me into decorating."

Danny grinned. "Well, all that's going to change soon."

"What do you mean?"

"The Gophers are coming to town."

"Your friends from high school?"

Danny laughed. "That's right. All four of them. Kyle, Hakeem, Jimmy, and Jose. They'll be here for a few days, and they're the ultimate guys' guys. They're a three-ring circus and once they get here, you'll be way too busy to worry about Elizabeth not having time for you. You're going to be booked solid."

Tom smiled. He'd heard hundreds of stories about the Gophers. They were a group of four guys who'd been friends since the first grade. They were wild. They were rugged. They played rugby. And they were fun with a capital *F*.

Tom began feeling a little better. Maybe spending some time with the guys was exactly what he needed. Aside from his roommate, Danny, Tom didn't really have any guy friends. Elizabeth had been the most important thing in his life for a long time now, and he was depending on her too much for emotional support and company.

It was time to stop being so clingy and needy. If Elizabeth was busy, she was busy. And he needed to get busy too.

"Amy," Elizabeth explained patiently. "If you won't tell your story, then I have no way to prove that Kitty's is guilty of discrimination."

"There's no way I'm going public with what happened to me. I'd be way too embarrassed. And I'd look like an idiot. People would say I'm jealous because I don't have a knockout body and that I'm trying to pull the plug on everybody's fun."

Elizabeth took a sip of her coffee and stared at Amy's humiliated face across the table in the Coffeecake Café. It was late morning, and the tables were full of people taking advantage of the low-priced serve-yourself Saturday brunch special.

She was tempted to ask the waiter for extra caffeine. She was completely exhausted, physically and mentally. Working at Kitty's was taking its toll. And so was the secrecy. Elizabeth was determined to tell Tom all about her investigation now.

If Amy wouldn't cooperate—and Elizabeth

133

didn't blame her—she really had no story to tell. Tom had more experience at making difficult stories work. Maybe he'd have some suggestions.

"I'll think of something," she said to Amy. "But right now, I'm going back up to the counter for another pastry. I need a sugar boost. How about you?"

Amy smiled forlornly. "What I need is a job. And a boost of self-esteem."

A lightbulb went on in Elizabeth's head. There was the story. The problem with places like Kitty's was that they set impossible standards of beauty for women, dooming them to a lifetime of low self-esteem.

But then again, so did fashion magazines and the movies.

Elizabeth groaned out loud. She definitely needed to talk to Tom.

"Excellent!" Mr. Guererro smiled broadly and applauded.

Billie bowed from her seated position, and he rewarded her with a delighted chuckle. "You *made* the time to practice," he said. "And you see how improved your playing is."

Mr. Guererro had called her this morning and asked if she could come in today since he had a dental appointment on the day of their next scheduled lesson. Thank goodness she'd followed through on her promise to practice. This time she wasn't caught unprepared.

He got up and went over to his desk, returning with a brochure. He handed it to her as he cleared his throat, sounding as if he had something important to say. "I must admit to you that I practiced a small piece of deception today."

"Deception?"

"I wanted to talk to you about something, but I needed to prove to myself first that you are . . . ummm . . . *qualified*. This was, how do you say it? A pop quiz." He chuckled again. "I do not have a dental appointment next week, but I wanted to hear how far you had come since our last lesson. I'm sorry to interrupt your Saturday, but I wanted to hear how well you could learn something in a short time."

Billie shook her head, feeling flattered but very confused. "I know that you are not a music major." He sat down in the chair across from her and leaned slightly forward, speaking intently. "But I think you should consider devoting a semester of your education to music if you can."

She shook her head. "That's impossible, Mr. Guererro. My parents pay my tuition and they'd never—"

He held up his hands, interrupting her. "Hear me out, please. This brochure is an application to compete in a guitar competition that will be held here, in our SVU auditorium, in a few days. The winner receives a free semester in Spain to study guitar with Señora Batista."

Billie gasped. Señora Batista was famous. She

135

was considered one of the finest classical guitarists in the world. Billie frowned over the brochure, reading rapidly through it. "But the competition is open to music majors only," she said.

"There is always latitude if the talent is great enough," he said significantly.

"What do you mean?"

"I mean that if you want to participate, I will attest to your level of skill and talent. On the strength of my recommendation, you would be allowed to compete. I am not Señora Batista, but I am not unknown in the world of music."

He was being modest. Though he rarely mentioned it, Billie knew he'd had a very promising concert career.

"You would do that for me?" Billie said in astonishment. "Why?"

He laughed again. "Because you are an extraordinary student. You have almost outgrown me, Billie. And I think that after a semester in Spain studying with Señora Batista, you could come back here and teach *me* a thing or two."

"I don't know what to say," Billie said, practically sputtering. Mr. Guererro had always been encouraging, but she had no idea that he had so much faith in her talent. It seemed ungrateful and stupid to say no to such a wonderful and flattering opportunity.

But it was impossible. Billie was supposed to graduate in two years and go right into a three-year law program. Everybody expected it. Her parents. *Steven*.

"Just think about it," Mr. Guererro encouraged.

*You don't just say to the great beyond, hey, thanks for the talent, but I think I'll take a pass. No. If you've got it, you're expected to use it. Or at least to try.*

Chas's words echoed in her ears. "If I did enter the competition," Billie asked slowly, "what would I play?"

Mr. Guererro's smile widened, and he sat back like a man who'd won a long and difficult argument. "The Bach," he said. "It's an excellent competition piece. But we need to work a little bit on . . . ummm . . ." He gave her a conspiratorial smile. "Showmanship."

"Showmanship? I thought serious musicians just worried about playing music."

"Serious musicians are serious competitors," he said. A steely glint appeared in the corner of his eye. "Welcome to show business. Now sit up straight and *smile*."

"You're late," Mr. Farley snapped from behind the jewelry counter. "This is the second time in four days." He was wiping the glass surface with the rag and bottle of ammonia cleaner that were kept on the bottom shelf.

Jessica hurried over to relieve him of this chore. Wiping down the counter was one of Jessica's many duties. She was supposed to do it when she arrived and before she left every shift. The counter

137

needed constant cleaning to keep it from looking smudged and dirty.

"I'm really sorry," Jessica said, taking the rag and bottle from him. "I had to stop for gas."

"On the store's time?" he asked dryly. "Ms. Wakefield . . ." He trailed off as a woman approached the jewelry counter and began perusing the contents. "We'll talk later," he said softly. "Please see to this customer, then come and find me."

Even though her heart was sinking into her shoes, Jessica forced herself to smile at the woman. "May I help you?" she asked brightly.

The woman didn't even bother to answer. She just continued walking along the length of the counter, looking down through the glass at the jewelry on display.

She was middle aged and wore an expensive suit made of woven mohair in spring colors. Heavy gold bangles and earrings complemented the ensemble well—even though the look was a little overdone, in Jessica's opinion. "What is the stone in that ring?" she asked abruptly, tapping impatiently on the counter with a long pink nail.

Just as she had been instructed, Jessica immediately unlocked the sliding door on her side of the display case and removed the ring. She placed it on the counter so that the woman could inspect it more closely and try it on if she chose.

"I didn't ask you to take it out," the woman snapped. "I just asked you what it was made of."

Jessica flushed. Very few people were rude, but

when they were, it was almost impossible not to be rude back. "The stone is carnelian," she answered.

"I've never heard of a carnelian," the woman said. "You must be mistaken. Go ask somebody who knows about these things."

Jessica took a deep breath. "Carnelian is a reddish brown quartz that comes from Japan, India, and some parts of South America," she explained patiently. "This particular piece came from Japan."

The woman gave Jessica an angry look. "I believe I requested that you go ask someone who knows more about these things."

"I don't need to ask somebody who knows," Jessica said, losing her temper. "Because *I* know. And the reason *I* know is because the jewelry buyer *told* me. Okay? If you want a second opinion, buy it and take it to the jewelry store. Then they can tell you the exact same thing I just told you."

"Ms. Wakefield," a voice thundered. "Would you step into my department, please?"

Jessica closed her eyes and ground her teeth. Mr. Farley seemed to have an almost supernatural ability for being within earshot every time she said or did something wrong. She gave the obnoxious woman a tight smile. "Excuse me." She put the ring back in the display case, shut it, locked it with a slam, and then walked toward Mr. Farley.

"What have I told you about courtesy?" he asked.

"Did you hear what she said to me?"

"Yes, I did. She's rude and obnoxious. She's a type who, unfortunately, entertains herself by abusing people she thinks are not in a position to abuse her back. And that's despicable. But none of that matters, Ms. Wakefield, because *she is a customer*. And if you want to make it in the world of retail, you learn that the unpalatable truth is *the customer is always right*. This is the third time you and I have had this conversation. If we have it again . . ."

Jessica felt like screaming. She was sick of being lectured to. She was sick of being threatened. She was sick of putting up with rude people. And she was sick of Mr. Farley. He seemed to be devoting his life to a nit-picking, bean-counting, statistical analysis of Jessica Wakefield's retail blunders, and she'd had enough!

The words *I quit* hovered on her lips. She longed to shout them. To scream them loud enough to blow Mr. Farley out of Women's Accessories, through Men's Casual, across Girls' Plus Sizes, and out the exit door.

The word *I* roiled in the back of her throat like bubbles rising in a pot of boiling water. But before she could utter the magic phrase that would free her from this horrible place, a rapid series of images froze the words in her mouth. She pictured Steven, placing so much faith in her that he was willing to gamble two months of servitude to Mike McAllery.

No way was she going to do that to Steven. And no way was she going to give Mike McAllery the satisfaction.

"I'll take care of the customer." Mr. Farley sighed. "You get some water and compose yourself." Then, to Jessica's amazement, he actually put a warm hand on her shoulder, as if he really did understand how difficult she was finding the job.

Somehow, the small gesture of kindness from such an unexpected supporter made her feel like crying. She rushed to the water fountain that was in a secluded corner of the store and bent over the fountain so that no one could see the tears in her eyes.

She felt another hand touch her elbow. "Rough day?"

Jessica straightened and did her best to smile at Val. She couldn't talk yet, but she nodded.

"This is a very tough business," Val said sympathetically. "You have to be a salesperson, a marketer, a stylist, a consultant, a politician, a psychologist, and a diplomat."

"I don't think I'm good enough at any of those things to—"

"Listen," Val said. "Hang in there until quitting time. Then come with me to the Fashion Arts Benefit."

"What's that?" Jessica asked, flattered to be asked to go anywhere with Val.

"It's a fashion show and fund-raiser for the

homeless," Val answered. "I've got two tickets. It's a major event. Lots of great clothes and fun people. Will you come?"

Jessica nodded, her bad mood quickly disappearing. She looked over toward the jewelry counter and watched Mr. Farley deal with the horrible woman. Even from the other side of the store, Jessica could hear the sharp staccato rudeness in the woman's demanding voice.

But Mr. Farley didn't get flustered. His face was a mask of amiability, and Jessica began to laugh. "How does he do it?" she asked.

Val winked. "He loves this business. And so do you, whether you know it yet or not. I know you don't like him, but he's one of the best salesmen I've ever seen. Come on, watch him and learn something."

"That price is absurd," the rude woman was complaining. "It's not even a precious stone."

Mr. Farley held the ring and wiped it delicately with a specially treated polishing cloth. "Man has always been willing to pay an absurd price for beauty and for skill," he said poetically. "This is more than a few ounces of silver and quartz. This is workmanship, design, and history." Satisfied that the ring could shine no brighter, he took her hand in a courtly style and put the ring on her finger. "Ahhh," he breathed. "A beautiful ring belongs on a beautiful hand."

The woman's unpleasant expression softened a bit. "It is very flattering."

Mr. Farley retained her hand, as if he couldn't stop admiring it. "You know, it's said that Muhammad wore a carnelian ring."

"Really?" the woman said.

"Oh, yes. And at one time, people believed that carnelian had special powers to protect them."

The woman removed her hand and held it up, scrutinizing the ring.

"Now how can we say the price is too high?" he asked lightly.

Jessica watched, astonished, as the woman produced a credit card. The next thing Jessica knew, the rude woman and Mr. Farley were chatting pleasantly while he wrote up her purchase.

"See," Val said. "I don't think I could have made that sale."

"I *know* I couldn't have," Jessica admitted.

"Someday you will," Val said. She put her bag under her arm. "Meet me at the employees' exit at seven," she said. "We'll take my car because the benefit's hard to find."

"How hard can it be?" Jessica asked.

"You'll see when we get there," Val promised.

Jessica wandered back over to the jewelry counter when the woman had walked away with a small Taylor's bag over her wrist. Mr. Farley was relocking the counter.

"Mr. Farley? You said you wanted to talk to me?"

Mr. Farley seemed distracted as he wiped down

the counter. "I remember the first customer who was rude to me," he said in a musing tone. "It was a man . . . I ended up jumping over the counter and punching him in the nose."

Jessica smiled. "And did your supervisor tell you to get some water and take over?"

He met Jessica's gaze. "No. He fired me on the spot. And that's how I learned *the hard way* that the customer is always right. If you're rude again, or late again, you're fired." He reached under the counter and found the rag and ammonia spray. "Clean off the counter, please."

He walked away, and Jessica ground her teeth. For a few brief moments, she'd begun to think Mr. Farley was actually human. But he wasn't. He was a monster, and if it weren't for Steven, she'd have told Mr. Farley exactly what she thought of him and his crummy job.

# *Chapter Ten*

Steven wiped the perspiration from his forehead as he finished his jog. Running up the stairs to the apartment, he opened the door and hurried past Billie, who was shuffling some papers. "Give me twenty minutes and I'll be ready to go," he panted.

"Go where?" she asked.

"To the sock hop," he said. "It's tonight."

Billie gave him a blank look, then smacked her forehead. "I forgot."

He smiled. "Better hurry and get dressed. I told Tom we'd meet him and Elizabeth at the dance and maybe grab a bite with them afterward."

Billie licked her lips and said nothing.

"Is there a problem? The dance starts really early, and I promise we won't be out late."

"I have to practice," she said, her voice slightly

antagonistic, as if she were expecting an argument.

"All night?" he asked.

"No. Not all night."

Steven felt his anger boiling. "Look. I know you have things to do, but I really need to spend some time with you. So will you please come with me?"

"I can't," she said abruptly. Billie clasped her hands together and wrung them as if she were agitated. "Steven, we have to talk," she said.

Steven felt his irritation turn to fear. "What?" he asked hoarsely, sure that she was about to tell him that she and Chas were madly in love and couldn't live without each other.

"I had a guitar lesson today."

Steven said nothing, watching her pale face.

"Mr. Guererro wants me to enter a competition being held in a few days. And that means a lot of practicing—starting tonight."

The relief was so overwhelming, Steven felt like laughing. His lips turned involuntarily in a goofy smile. "Billie, I think that's great! I'm really proud of you. Will there be an audience? Can I see you play?"

Billie nodded. "Yes. It'll be in the auditorium of the music building. There will be a lot of people. And judges."

He got up and put his arms around her. He knew he was sweaty, but he just had to hold her. "I'll be in the front row," he promised, trying hard to sound as if he sincerely believed this was

146

the greatest thing he'd ever heard. If Billie wanted to spend her time tinkering with electives, that was fine. Anything she wanted to do was fine, as long as she didn't run off with another guy. "So what do you win?" he asked. "Money? A new guitar? Tickets to a concert?"

"A semester in Spain," she answered. "To study with Señora Batista. She's a very famous musician."

Steven felt his heart give a huge thump. He released her and stepped back. "A semester in Spain?" he repeated.

Billie met his eyes squarely but said nothing.

"You're going to Spain?"

"The *winner* goes to Spain," she said softly.

Steven began walking in a large circle around the apartment, trying to keep from shouting. "So let me get this straight . . . I think it's safe to assume that since you're entering the competition, you hope to win it. Right? And if you win, you'll be moving to Spain. Right? And if you move to Spain, then obviously we're no longer together."

"Steven," she began with a catch in her voice.

"Right?" he repeated in a savage tone. "Answer me, Billie. What is it you're trying to tell me?"

"This isn't a courtroom!" she shouted at the top of her voice. "This is my life. *My* life, Steven. Meaning it belongs to me. Billie Winkler. And *I* get to make some decisions about it. Whether they meet with your approval or not."

He gasped. He'd never heard Billie raise her

voice. But now she stood in front of him red-faced with fury, tears of anger streaming down her cheeks.

"This isn't about whether or not I approve," he bellowed back. "Quit trying to make me out to be some overbearing monster. This is about you making a decision about breaking up and—"

"Who said anything about breaking up?" she yelled.

He stared at her. "You're talking about leaving me," he said in a slow, patient tone, as if he were trying to explain something very simple to a child. "If you're on one continent and I'm on another, it's kind of hard to maintain a relationship."

"I knew you were going to react like this," she said angrily, reaching into her pocket for a tissue. "I can't talk to you about anything anymore."

"I'm out of here," Steven announced. He stormed back out the door and thundered down the steps, beginning a second run. Maybe when he got back, Billie would be ready to talk about this thing logically.

As Steven crossed the parking lot he saw Mike waxing the '57 Thunderbird. Mike waved at him, but Steven was too upset to stop and talk.

He pumped his arms, picking up speed as he headed back toward the track that circled the park. Spain. *Spain.* Where was all this coming from? Overnight their life together had fallen apart.

Obviously the thought of being separated from him for a semester wasn't bothering Billie a bit.

But the thought of being away from her was so awful and painful, Steven's knees almost buckled. If he lost Billie, he wouldn't know what to do. He loved her and he didn't want to lose her.

The thing to do was run until he was so worn out, he'd stop being so angry. Then he'd try to talk to Billie quietly and see if they couldn't work all this out.

Billie dried her tears and went over to the sink to splash some cool water on her face. They'd both been too emotional to make sense. She needed to calm down, get a grip, and try to talk rationally to Steven when he got back.

She patted her face dry with a dish towel, opened a window, and then went into the living room and reached for her guitar. Billie began running through some of the exercises she'd committed to memory.

Soon her fingers were flying over the strings like a professional's. But she wasn't a professional, she reminded herself. She wasn't even a music major. And the exercise she was playing was just that—an exercise. A beginning exercise at that.

She and Steven were getting all emotional over something that was only a remote possibility. She didn't have a shot at winning, but she still wanted to compete. Billie had never given a recital or played in public. An event like this would give her experience in performing and working toward a deadline.

Billie began to feel better. When Steven returned, she'd explain things so that he wouldn't feel as threatened. She heard footsteps climb the outside steps and put the guitar away, running to the door to greet Steven. She threw it open. "Oh!"

Chas smiled. "Don't stop playing on my account. I could hear you from the court downstairs." He had some books of music under his arm. He frowned. "You look strange. Have you been crying? Is this a bad time to drop in?"

"Steven and I had a fight," she said, stepping back and inviting him in.

"Nothing to do with me, I hope," Chas said anxiously.

"I'm entering a guitar competition," she explained. "If I win, I'll go to Spain for a semester."

"That's amazing," Chas said happily. "Good luck. It'll be so cool if you win because I'll be studying in France next year. We could get together in Paris. Or maybe Barcelona."

She smiled. "That would be fun. But I doubt I'll win. And I hope I don't. Because life will be very complicated if I do."

Chas put the music down on the coffee table. "Don't get me wrong. I think you're very talented and I think you could go a long way, but—" He broke off and flushed.

"But what?"

"This is going to sound mean, and I hope you'll take it the right way, but I wouldn't worry too much about winning."

In spite of herself, Billie began to laugh. "Well, thanks a lot!" she retorted.

"I don't mean it the way it sounds. Win or lose, competitions are great experiences. But there are so many things that affect whether you win or lose. And if you let winning or losing be the barometer of your talent, you're going to wind up a soggy mass of artistic insecurity. Take it from a veteran of about a thousand competitions. I've lost a whole lot more than I've won. The point is—don't put too much pressure on it. Prepare, but don't stop living in the meantime."

She patted him on the shoulder. "You've just put my exact thoughts into words."

He sat down on the couch. "Well, after what you've told me, you're probably not interested in any new work, but let's look over some of these pieces anyway. When the competition's over, maybe we can work on that duet we talked about. Hey, are you and Steven going to the sock hop? Mickey's going and a bunch of people from the music department will be there."

Billie didn't really want to go, but since Steven did, going might be a first step toward mending the damage between them. "I think so," she said. "I'll check with Steven when he gets back."

"Great." Chas pushed up the sleeves of his blue work shirt and began leafing through the books he'd brought.

A few minutes later they were laughing and chatting, turning the pages on music that Billie

151

knew she could never sight read. "Four flats!" she exclaimed. "No way. That key is too hard."

"Oh, come on," Chas argued. "Be a sport. How do you know you can't sight read it if you don't try?"

The door slammed and they both jumped. Billie hadn't heard Steven come in and now he stood in the doorway, giving her and Chas a flat look.

Chas stood and smiled. "Hey, Steven, good to see you."

Steven nodded, and Billie took a deep breath. "Steven, Chas wants to go to the sock hop. So maybe we should go."

"I went last year," Chas said. "It was a major blast, and the DJ was great. Believe it or not, I like rock and roll." He laughed, working hard to diffuse Steven's obvious anger. "Just wanted you to know that in case you thought I was a total loser. It's sort of an occupational hazard when you're a music major."

Billie laughed, but Steven didn't. "I'll take a shower," he said curtly, walking into the bedroom and closing the door.

Chas looked at Billie. "Did I say something wrong again?"

Billie shook her head. "No. It has nothing to do with you. Don't worry. He'll be fine." *I hope,* she added mentally.

Steven's face looked more rigid now than it had before he'd left. Billie had imagined them

152

calmly talking things through, but it was obvious from Steven's stony expression that it wasn't going to be that simple. She'd have to make a major effort at the sock hop.

Steven turned the water on hard, letting it pummel his back. When he wanted to go to the dance, Billie had to practice. But now that *Chas* wanted to go, practicing wasn't as important.

Things were getting clearer and clearer every second.

"This is a fashion show!" Jessica exclaimed as she and Val threaded their way through the asphalt parking lot, carefully walking through puddles in their high-heeled shoes.

They were in a part of town full of commercial buildings, warehouses, and industrial-use spaces. There were few streetlights. If there hadn't been two hundred cars parked in the lot and people crowding around a brightly lit warehouse, Jessica would have suggested that they skip it and go home. This looked like a great place to get mugged.

"Yup, this is a fashion show," Val confirmed with a laugh.

They approached the building with a sign over the door that said ACE WELDING. "What are they modeling?" Jessica asked. "Goggles and hard hats?"

Val smiled. "This is where the avant-garde happens. By the time you see something on a runway in Paris or Milan, it's already come and gone in this world. This is the front line of trendy. It's not wearable. And it's not really sellable, either. But it's fun. Come on."

Outside the building an odd collection of people stood chatting. A woman in a fake fur leopard jacket held a poodle that had been painted to match the jacket. Both the dog and the woman had long cigarette holders in their mouths. Talking with the woman was a middle-aged man with a hunter green mohawk and a business suit. But on his feet he wore slippers that curled up at the toes like elf shoes.

Inside there were Elvis look-alikes, punks, grungers, and sleek-looking women wearing little black dresses and chignons at the backs of their necks.

The warehouse was dark, littered with equipment, and rigged with bright, glaring lights that made the interior look blue, smoky, and slightly sinister. A white-jacketed waiter appeared with a tray of sparkling water and another one appeared with a tray of hors d'oeuvres.

Val took a glass and something round with an olive and smiled her thanks at the waiters. "What do you think?"

"I'm blown away," Jessica said. "Where's the runway?"

Val pointed across the warehouse at the catwalk along the second floor. "I'm guessing there."

Right on cue loud, rhythmic rock music began blaring. Bright lights illuminated the metal catwalk, and the entire crowd turned in that direction and looked upward.

The air was electric and when the first model came striding across the catwalk, hips swaying, head tossing, and dress twirling, Jessica involuntarily began to applaud.

The music. The lights. The setting. The mood. It was the hippest thing Jessica had ever attended. A second model, tall and dark skinned, came striding across. Her high heels made her look almost like a giant. Her boxy jacket looked as if it had been constructed from cardboard. She pivoted, removing it in a graceful, fluid movement to reveal a dress underneath that was made of something shiny, silver, and textured like the cardboard.

It was becoming obvious that there was a theme—incorporating the textures and colors of industrial materials into fashion.

One model after another appeared, and some of them *did* wear hard hats and welding masks with outrageously far-out clothes.

Every new dress was a surprise. There was humor. There was style. And there was sophistication. Jessica glanced around at the crowd. There weren't too many people her own age in here. She was probably the youngest.

Suddenly her eyes rested on a familiar face. A face that was looking directly at her.

What in the world was Mike McAllery doing here?

Jessica, sure he was staring at her, couldn't help feeling slightly gratified that he was watching her when there were so many gorgeous models to watch.

The show didn't last long, and when the model dressed as a bride closed the show, wearing a gown dotted with Styrofoam packing peanuts instead of the traditional pearls, Jessica applauded loudly along with the rest of the audience.

A young man dressed all in black with his hair greased back into a ponytail ran out to the center of the catwalk, took a bow, and then suddenly, it was all over.

The lights snapped off. The music stopped, and people began to chat. Jessica saw Mike move in a straight line toward her and Val. She smiled as he approached, but before she could say a word, Val stepped forward. "Mike!" she cried.

Mike hugged her and kissed her cheek. "I kept trying to catch your eye," he said. "But you didn't see me."

"Great show," she commented.

"Yeah. These things are always fun." His eyes floated past Jessica, and then he did a double take. "Jessica! I didn't see you." He gave her a party kiss and a warm handshake, as if she were an old friend. "And it's always nice to see my ex-wife."

Jessica felt a surge of irritation. Mike McAllery hadn't been staring across the room at her. He'd been staring across the room at Val. "How long have you two known each other?" she asked.

Val threw back her head and laughed. A deep, throaty laugh that implied a backlog of private jokes, shared memories, and double sets of snapshots. "Don't tell her. It'll make me feel old."

Mike put an arm around Val's shoulders. "You look as fabulous as ever." He turned to Jessica. "So what did you think of the show?"

"I loved it. What did you think? I never knew you were interested in fashion."

Mike tugged at an earlobe. "I'm interested in a lot of things." It seemed to Jessica that he and Val exchanged a significant look.

Jealousy, unbidden and unjustified, threatened to spoil her evening. Obviously Mike and Val had some kind of relationship.

But she didn't care, Jessica reminded herself sternly. She liked Val. And she hoped Val didn't have any illusions about Mike. If she did, she could get hurt in a big way.

*Should I say anything?* she wondered. No. If she did, Val would just think she was jealous.

Val was old enough to take care of herself. And—thankfully—Mike McAllery's personal life was none of Jessica's business anymore.

# *Chapter Eleven*

"Great sound system," Mickey commented, his long hair swaying as his shoulders moved slightly to the beat.

"Hey, Steven," Isabella said as she and Danny twirled past Steven and Mickey, joining the throng of dancers in the center of the large room. Lots of them wore fifties-style clothing. Denise and Winston had on matching bowling shirts.

Steven saw Alexandra Rollins, Elizabeth's friend from high school, wearing a poodle skirt with her hair pulled up in a ponytail at the top of her head. She was dancing with a guy wearing an argyle sweater with a bow tie.

Huge cardboard records decorated the walls and hung from the ceiling. And everybody wore sneakers. The atmosphere was all vintage nineteen fifties.

But apparently this Mickey guy hadn't gotten

the word. He looked like he had stepped right out of the sixties.

"I love this music," Mickey shouted over the noise.

Steven wished Mickey would get lost. Just looking at him annoyed Steven. Long hair was so affected. And he was wearing one of those stupid collarless shirts that looked even more affected. As far as Steven was concerned, the only men who looked normal in shirts like that were Amish. The music stopped, and the dancing couples seemed to be waiting for the next song.

"So, Steven, I hear you're an economics major too." Mickey lifted his glass of punch to his lips.

"You got a problem with that?" Steven demanded in a hostile tone.

Mickey's eyes widened behind his glasses and he froze, his cup hovering in front of his lips. "Did I say something wrong?" he asked.

"No. But your question sounded more like an opinion than a request for information."

Mickey smiled tightly. "I'm sorry if that's the impression you got. I was just trying to make conversation."

Steven turned away, and his eyes found Billie on the dance floor. The music had started again, and she and Chas were laughing as they danced, trying silly steps that didn't match the music, bumping into the couples around them.

They weren't passionately holding on to each other, but what they were doing seemed somehow intimate. Billie looked happier and more at ease with Chas than she ever did with Steven.

"I'm sorry," he muttered at Mickey. "I'm just in a bad mood. I think I need to be alone." He strode toward the exit, pushed it open, and stood in the alley, taking deep breaths and trying to calm a rising sense of panic and misery.

The music sounded as if it were coming from far away, and he wished he could shut out the sound completely. Steven couldn't help picturing Billie and Chas moving to the beat, standing closer and closer.

After what seemed like an eternity, the song ended and another one began. Steven knew the song very well. He listened to the first verse, feeling as if his heart were breaking.

"There you are." He turned and saw Billie standing behind him. "I've been looking for you. They're playing our song."

Steven looked up at the sky. She was humoring him now. Trying to pretend, at least for tonight, that there was nothing wrong.

"Will you come in and dance with me?" she asked in a soft voice.

"I don't feel much like dancing," he answered. "This party isn't as fun as I thought it would be."

"Just this one dance," she urged. "Then if you want, we can leave."

"Suit yourself," he said abruptly, taking her arm and walking back into the gym.

"So what do you say?" Tom asked. "Want to get something to eat afterward with Steven and Billie?"

161

Elizabeth leaned against Tom's chest—literally. She was so pooped, she felt as if she could hardly stand up straight. "I'd really rather go someplace where we can talk," she said.

He looked down at her and smiled. "Wow! I'm flattered. You actually want to spend some time alone with me?"

"I'm sorry I've been so busy. When we get someplace private, I'll explain more about . . ."

"Hey," he said in a soft voice. "No explanations necessary. All I want is some time alone with my favorite woman—who has obviously spent too much time hitting the books. Did you know you have circles under your eyes? Not that I'm complaining. It's a very becoming shade of violet."

"Ha, ha," she said sarcastically, snuggling her cheek in the hollow of his shoulder. Tom's arms tightened around the small of her back, and nothing had ever felt so good in her entire life. Her back ached almost as much as her feet.

Mr. O'Connor had been right. There were busboys to bring out the really heavy trays. But the waitresses were still expected to carry the light stuff and remain on their feet for hours at a time.

Elizabeth closed her eyes and did some mental calculations. She figured she made at least two hundred trips a night between the kitchen and her station. She tried to convert the distance into yards and the yards into miles and then began to feel guilty.

Glenda was there tonight. Shorthanded and probably making three times that many trips to the kitchen. Even though Elizabeth didn't care about Kitty's, she did feel a certain loyalty to Glenda.

*Get a grip, Liz,* she said to herself. *You've got to stop thinking about Kitty's until you talk to Tom after the dance.*

The music switched from a soft, romantic ballad to a pounding rock-and-roll classic. She and Tom parted and began moving separately to the music.

She looked up to smile at him and noticed that his eyes were focused on something a few yards away. She followed the direction of his gaze and came to a stop.

He was watching another woman. A woman with lots of curves in all the right places. Curves that were moving up and down and side to side with the music.

Tom seemed suddenly to notice that Elizabeth wasn't dancing. He tore his eyes away and turned them toward her.

When he saw her outraged face, he blushed a fiery red. Elizabeth could see him mentally scrambling to think of something to say. Well, whatever he had to say, she wasn't interested in hearing it.

She turned and stormed toward the front doors. She hadn't wanted to come to this silly dance anyway. And she sure wasn't going to stick around while Tom—

"Elizabeth!" He grabbed her arm and pulled her to a stop in the middle of the quadrangle.

"I thought you were different," she spat. "I really did. I can't believe you'd do something so . . . so . . . so offensive."

"I'm really sorry," Tom said. "I am different, Liz. I really am. You know I'm not an offensive jerk. I'm a man . . . and men like to look, although sometimes we're not as discreet as we should be, and . . ."

Elizabeth broke away. There was no excuse for his behavior. She wasn't going to let him off the hook. Everybody was capable of changing their behavior if it upset somebody else—and that included Tom Watts.

"Come on, Lila. Let's go to the dance."

Lila didn't move. She just sat there in the chair by Bruce's window, her chin resting on her folded arms, staring gloomily out into the night.

She was obviously miserable, and Bruce racked his brains for some plan to entertain or cheer her up. He went over and stooped next to her. "It'll be fun. Come on," he said, trying to cheer her out of her bad mood. "How about we head over to the university center, find some of your buddies, and . . ."

She lifted her head and glared at him. "Stop it!" she hissed angrily. "Stop talking to me in that tone of voice. Stop humoring me. I'm not a child."

"Who's talking to you like you were a child?" he protested.

"You are. So cut it out. I get enough of that from my dad." She turned her face back toward the window and settled her chin firmly back on her arms.

The music changed again. This time it was a ballad Billie didn't recognize. Billie enjoyed the feel of

Steven's arms around her. It had been a long time since they'd danced slowly to something romantic.

She tightened her arms around Steven's shoulders, but his arms didn't tighten around her waist and his back remained rigid. He was angry. And coming to the dance hadn't helped.

She sighed heavily, wishing she'd never told him about the competition. Chas was right. She wasn't going to win. She'd just started a big fight for nothing.

But these days, it seemed as if big fights were starting over nothing all the time.

Suddenly and without warning, Billie's stomach turned over and she felt like she was about to get sick. Jerking away from Steven, she pressed her hands to her mouth. In less than two minutes she was sure she was going to throw up.

Billie raced to the exit, pushing it open. She ran into the alley and found a secluded place behind the garbage cans where she could retch quietly.

"Billie! Billie! What's wrong?" Steven stood beside her and held her hair back with one hand while fumbling in his pocket for a napkin.

She took it gratefully and wiped her lips. She felt queasy and dizzy, and her face was bathed in a cold sweat. "I think we'd better go home," she said, breathing deeply to counteract the nausea.

He took her arm. "Sure. Let's go right now. I hope you're okay. Think it's the flu?"

She shook her head. "No. I think it's stress. I

just think the stress of our relationship is making me sick."

Steven stopped and gaped at her. "The stress of our relationship is making you sick," he repeated in disbelief.

"Yes!" she said, beginning to cry. "And please quit acting like every concern I have is ridiculous and insulting."

"That *is* ridiculous and I *am* insulted," he said angrily. "You know, Billie," he said sarcastically. "I never noticed any *stress* before Chas and guitar lessons seemed to take over our whole lives."

"That's because I did everything your way," she said resentfully. "Now I'm starting to make decisions on my own and you can't handle it. You can't handle me having friends. You can't handle me having interests that don't interest you. And you can't handle the far-fetched possibility that we might spend a few months apart. And you know what? *I* can't handle that."

"Wait here," Steven said between gritted teeth. "And I'll go get the car. Think you can handle that? Or would you rather get the car yourself? It's *your* decision. I certainly wouldn't want to make up your mind for you."

# Chapter Twelve

"What are you doing home so early?" Jessica asked when Elizabeth came hurrying in the door. "I thought you'd be at the dance."

Elizabeth angrily threw her purse on the bed. "I was at the dance. But I had a fight with Tom."

"A fight? About what?"

Elizabeth's lips opened and closed a few times, and then she shook her head. "Never mind. It's too hard to explain." She sat down on the bed and gave Jessica a long look. "Just as well. We haven't had much time to hang out together. So how's work going?"

Jessica walked over to her bureau and picked up a nail file. She was still dressed and charged up after the fashion show. But at the same time, she felt gloomy. "Good and bad," she answered. "I went to a fashion show tonight with somebody at work."

"Great. Was it fun?"

"Yeah. But seeing all that high-tech, high-fashion, avant-garde glamour makes Taylor's look like bargain basement city."

"Hey, you've gotta start somewhere," Elizabeth responded with a strained laugh.

Jessica tapped on her nail. "Yeah, but that's not what's bothering me."

"So what is?"

"I think the person I went to the fashion show with is fooling around with Mike."

"Mike McAllery?"

"Yeah. He was there." Briefly Jessica filled her sister in on Val Tripler.

"So Mike was at a fashion show and spoke to Val? That doesn't mean they're dating."

"Val is smart and ambitious, but she's sticking around that crummy old store full of moldy merchandise. Why isn't she working for some trendy, cutting-edge fashion company in L.A.?"

"You think she's here because of Mike?"

"Maybe."

"So what do you care?" Elizabeth asked, her voice neutral.

"I don't," Jessica responded truthfully. "But I don't want to be at Taylor's when Mike comes roaring up on his motorcycle to pick her up. And I don't want Mike to watch while Mr. Farley spends all his free time yelling at me."

"So quit," Elizabeth said succinctly. "The last thing you need right now is aggravation."

Jessica picked up her purse and headed for the door.

"I didn't mean now," Elizabeth said with a laugh.

Jessica smiled. "I'm not going to Taylor's. I'm going to Steven's. And Elizabeth . . ."

"Yeah?"

"Thanks for listening." She closed the door and walked quickly down the steps to the first floor.

She couldn't quit before she talked to Steven. *He'll figure out a way for me to quit without letting Mike win the bet.*

Steven opened the door, and Billie skirted past him into the dark apartment without a word. They'd driven home in angry silence.

He wanted to say something. Something that would ease the situation. But things had gotten way out of hand. He turned on the light, and Billie marched straight into the bedroom and slammed the door shut.

Well, that was a pretty clear signal. Obviously Billie wasn't going to make any effort to ease the situation either. Steven kicked off his shoes and got a spare pillow from the hall closet. If he was sleeping on the couch, he might as well turn in now—not that he was going to sleep a wink.

"I blew it. I haven't seen Liz for days, and then I act like some high school loser." Tom ran his

169

hands through his hair. He felt like pulling it out by the handful.

The whole night had fallen apart. Steven and Billie had left the dance practically ten minutes after they'd arrived. They'd obviously had some kind of fight too. Maybe there was something in the air . . . or a full moon.

"Relax, man," Danny urged, his arm around Isabella's shoulder. "You hurt her feelings, but you apologized. She'll be ready to make up tomorrow."

"I don't think so," Tom fretted. "Isabella, you're a woman. Tell me what to do. How do I make this right?"

Isabella laughed and took a sip of her soda. The three were standing outside on the quadrangle. The night was cool, and inside the university center the sock hop rocked on. The music filtered out toward them. "Well, you shouldn't wait until tomorrow to make up. Go over there now and bring her flowers."

"I've already tried that once."

"So try it again," Isabella advised. "Just leave them outside her door or something. Let her know you're thinking about her and that you're trying to make up."

Tom didn't even bother to say good night. He just took off and ran for the parking lot.

There was no traffic, and it took Jessica only a few minutes to reach Steven's apartment complex.

She parked the Jeep, let herself in the gate, and hurried toward Steven's apartment door, zipping her bomber jacket against the night air.

As she started up the steps, Jessica saw the light in Steven's living room go out. "Oh!" An involuntary cry of disappointment escaped her.

"You should try calling first. This is the second time you've come by too late to drop in." The voice in the dark was warm and seductive.

Jessica whirled and saw Mike sitting in a chair beside the pool. She looked around quickly for signs of Val, but he appeared to be alone.

"Fun show tonight," he said, standing up and slouching toward her. "But you know what?"

"What?"

"Of all the women in that room, the best-looking one was . . ."

"Val Tripler?" she ventured with a tight smile.

He chuckled and ran a hand through his hair. "You'll never change, will you?"

She let out a laugh of disbelief. "*I'll* never change."

"Okay, okay. I'm not exactly a changed man either. But what I was going to say was that the best-looking woman there was you." Mike took her hand and pulled her slightly toward the shadows. "I don't know what you came to talk to your big brother about," he said. "But if you want to talk to your ex-husband, I'm all ears."

"I don't think so," she said coldly, pulling her hand away.

He laughed knowingly. "You want to quit that job, don't you?"

She didn't answer, and he laughed again. "Well, if you're going to quit, it would be great if you'd do it this week. I could really use Steven's help. Waxing all those cars by myself is eating into my free time."

Jessica turned on her heel and marched back toward the parking lot. She was fuming as she climbed into the Jeep.

Nothing Steven could say or do was going to change the terms of their bet now. Not when Mike was so obviously eager to see her fail. If she quit or got fired now, Mike would hold Steven to the bet just to rub it in.

Why did she have to learn everything the hard way? It was great having Steven look after her. Give her advice. Boost her self-esteem. Make decisions for her. But she knew now that from here on, she'd do better to make decisions on her own.

The phone rang, and Elizabeth reached for it. "Hello?"

She heard music blasting in the background. "Elizabeth? It's Glenda. Gilly's a no-show, so now we're out three girls. Is there any way you could come in tonight?"

Elizabeth groaned.

"I wouldn't ask if I didn't need you. But you know what Saturday nights are like."

Glenda had been enormously helpful, generous

with advice, and quick to help out if Elizabeth's station was crowded. Elizabeth owed her a favor. "Sure," she said. "Just let me get dressed and I'll be there in half an hour."

Elizabeth hung up, groaning again. She went to her drawer and fished out the underwire push-up bra and spongy pads that she used to make her chest look bigger.

She arranged the whole contraption, feeling a little like a horse getting into harness, and pulled on a T-shirt. She was just reaching for her coat when she heard something in the hallway. A rustling sound.

Quietly she moved toward the door and pressed her ear against it. Yep. There was definitely somebody out there. And if they'd had any legitimate reason for being there, they would have knocked.

The last few months Elizabeth's life had been packed with danger and drama, and she felt a rising surge of anger. Somebody was probably playing a practical joke, trying to worry her.

It could be Winston, she thought irritably. He loved practical jokes but sometimes didn't think them through.

Well, it was time to let whoever it was know that she wasn't in the mood for any practical jokes, no matter how well-intentioned. She grabbed the knob and jerked open the door.

To her shock and surprise, Tom came flying into the room with a yelp of surprise. Yellow and

173

pink flowers fell in every direction, and white baby's breath flew upward like the spray of a fountain as Tom stumbled over her desk chair and landed in a sprawled heap on the floor.

"Tom! What were you doing outside my door?"

He sat up and gave her a sheepish look. "I was trying to surprise you with some flowers. I wanted to leave them on your doorknob with a card."

"Well, you surprised me all right," she said in a dry voice. She leaned over to pick up the flowers and heard him suck in his breath with a shocked gasp. She looked up to see what had caught his attention and saw that his eyes were riveted to her chest.

She began to blush furiously and straightened up.

"L-Liz," he sputtered, climbing to his feet. "What have I done to you?" He took her hands. "Please, please don't think I want you to change anything like . . . like . . ." He trailed off in embarrassment, unsure how to politely articulate what he was trying to say.

Elizabeth's mouth opened and closed. She knew what Tom was thinking—that somehow his interest in that girl's figure had prompted her to make changes in her own appearance.

"Forget the flowers," he sputtered, thrusting something into her hand. "Just read the card."

Feeling very silly, she opened the large pink card. On the front flap there was a picture of two hands clasped together, one male, one female. The male hand was pressing a rose into the female hand.

She opened the card and read the inscription. "I love you just the way you are." Tom had underlined the motto and added a series of exclamation points in red ink.

Elizabeth didn't know whether to laugh or cry. Tom was gazing at her with so much apologetic uncertainty that she couldn't find it in her heart to stay mad at him.

She lifted her arms and he stepped into her embrace, wrapping his arms around her waist.

"I'm so sorry," he said.

"It's okay," she murmured. "Let's not talk about it anymore."

"Fine by me," he agreed quickly with a sigh of relief. "How about celebrating our making up with something chocolate and a cup of coffee at the Canteen?"

"Um, I've got a major headache," Elizabeth lied. "But I'll call you tomorrow."

"That's the oldest kiss-off line in the world," he protested.

She laughed and pushed him out the door. "I mean it," she promised. "But right now . . ." Elizabeth put her fingers to her temples and feigned distress. "I really just need some sleep."

"Sure," Tom said quickly, eager to please and compromise. "You call me when you're ready. Anytime. Day or night."

She laughed and shut the door. Then she waited. She'd give him five minutes to clear out of the lobby, then she'd head for Kitty's.

Elizabeth leaned her forehead against the door as she listened to the sound of his footsteps disappearing down the hall. Tom had made all the appropriate gestures of apology. And he'd said all the right things—the things he knew she wanted to hear.

But she knew that deep down, it would be impossible for him to understand that what was going on at Kitty's wasn't just an opportunity for guys who liked to look.

Elizabeth wished she'd never started this investigation. She felt completely alone. Nobody was going to help her put a stop to what was going on. After tonight, she had to quit. Because right now it seemed as if the only support she was going to get on this thing was made of wire and foam rubber.

# Chapter Thirteen

Billie felt it coming the minute her eyes opened. "Out of my way!" she groaned.

Steven was walking out of the bathroom after his shower as she barreled past him and slammed the door with only seconds to spare.

Billie vomited into the toilet bowl, feeling as if the entire contents of her stomach were about to come up. This was the second time this week. It couldn't be the flu. She didn't have any fever.

After a few agonizing minutes in the bathroom Billie felt marginally better. Just as she expected, Steven was standing outside the door, his arms crossed and his face glowering.

"Stop looking at me like that," she snapped.

"Like what?"

"Like me being sick is some kind of personal insult."

"It *is* a personal insult," he responded. "You *told* me I was making you sick."

"I didn't mean it that way," she muttered, pushing past him and heading for the kitchen.

She heard Steven close the bathroom door with an angry slam. In the kitchen Billie slowly poured herself a glass of cold water. Maybe he was right. Maybe it was the stress of the competition that was getting to her. At first winning had seemed like such a remote possibility, it had been hard to take the argument seriously.

But after three days of intense practice she'd come to the realization that she desperately wanted to win. And she desperately wanted to make music her life. Every time she contemplated the thought of losing, it made her heartsick.

Billie closed the refrigerator door and saw a picture of herself and Steven that had been taken at a picnic several weeks ago. It had been a gorgeous day. One of those California afternoons that combined summery warmth and a crispy breeze.

Billie and Steven had spent the afternoon with another couple at a park. As the other couple had argued and bickered all day, Billie had realized she was an incredibly lucky woman. Steven was everything she'd ever dreamed about in a man.

He was funny, intelligent, handsome, and helplessly in love with her.

How could so much have changed in such a short time? Now she felt smothered. Dissatisfied. Misunderstood. Victimized, even. As if she had to hide her real interests and abilities in order to meet with Steven's approval.

She snatched the photo from the refrigerator. "I will win," she said to the picture of Steven. "And you can't stop me, Steven Wakefield."

"You're her best friend," Bruce insisted.

"I still can't help you," Jessica said. "And Mr. Farley will be back from lunch in fifteen minutes," she warned. "If he sees you here, you'll get thrown out and I'll get fired."

"I'm a paying customer," he argued.

"You haven't bought anything yet," she snapped, arranging the belts so that they hung in a more accessible place.

"You can't say I haven't tried," he said. "Come on, Jessica. Please help me. You must have *some* idea about what I could buy Lila that would cheer her up."

Jessica eyed the belts and held one up. "Here. It's the most expensive one we have."

Bruce took it from her hand, examined the price tag, and handed it back to her. "It's not expensive enough."

"I can mark it up if you want me to."

"Jessica, get serious. Lila's way down in the dumps."

"Aren't we all," Jessica said sourly.

"I need to get her something that will take her mind off her troubles."

"Look," Jessica said in a brusque tone. "I'd

179

love to help you, Bruce. And I'd love to sell you something really expensive and get the commission. But you know as well as I do that nothing in this store is going to cheer Lila up. There's nothing in *any* store. I mean, what does Lila want that Lila doesn't have?"

"A direction," Bruce answered. "A job. A focus."

"You can't buy that for her," Jessica said.

Bruce sighed heavily. "I know. So what am I supposed to do? I love her, but she's so totally down it's making *me* feel totally down."

Jessica straightened the belt rack. "You're a nice boyfriend, Bruce. I wish somebody would worry about me the way you worry about Lila."

Bruce put an arm around her. "Hey, Jessica, I'm sorry. I've just gone on and on about me and Lila. I know you're having a rough time too." He dropped his voice. "Just between you and me, are you having some kind of financial problem? Because if you are, I could help out with a loan. You don't have to keep working in this dump if you don't want to."

Jessica smiled and squeezed his arm. "Thanks. But I'm not working because of the money."

"It's the self-esteem thing, right?" Bruce threw up his hands. "See? Everybody's into it. I've got to do something for Lila."

"Whatever you do, please do it someplace else." Jessica turned him around and pushed him toward the side door. "Because here comes trouble."

180

Bruce looked over his shoulder and caught a glimpse of that Farley dude coming in the front door. He quickened his steps toward the exit. Farley was nuts, and Bruce didn't want another encounter with Taylor's security force.

Outside on the sidewalk he saw people hurrying to and fro on their way back from lunch. Good-looking, well-dressed men and women hurrying into office buildings and stores.

Bruce leaned against the wall. If working in an office or a store was the way to self-esteem, then Lila wasn't ever going to have any. For that matter, neither was he.

They weren't the kind of people who did things the way everybody else did. They were different. They were rich. They liked to write their own rules and do their own thing.

He watched a couple of motorcycles pull up in front of the IceHouse across the street. Two grungy-looking motorcycle guys removed their helmets, revealing bald, tattooed heads. They plopped the helmets on the handlebars, dismounted like cowboys, and wandered into the IceHouse behind two preppie-looking sorority girls and a long-haired musician type.

Bruce thought about going over for a cola and checking out the scene, but he felt too restless—and for the first time slightly worried about his own future as well as Lila's.

What was going to happen to them after college? Sure, right now life was full of classes and parties. But what were they going to do all day when their friends were working at real jobs? He continued walking down the street, and on the next block a Help Wanted sign in the window of a doughnut shop caught his eye.

*What does Lila want that Lila doesn't have?*

Bruce looked up the street at the crowd outside the IceHouse. Then he looked at the doughnut shop again.

He looked at the IceHouse.

He looked at the doughnut shop.

IceHouse.

Doughnut shop.

IceHouse.

Doughnut shop.

*Hmm.*


"Party! Party! Party!"

Tom laughed. Danny's friends *were* rowdy. Jimmy, Kyle, Hakeem, and Jose had arrived wearing matching green-and-black rugby shirts. The minute they entered the room with their sleeping bags and backpacks, Tom felt as if somebody had thrown a human grenade into their midst.

He and Danny were both big guys. Add another four big guys with loud voices and a colorful vocabulary, and their dorm room began to feel awfully small.

"I know they're a little *loud*," Danny whispered, "but trust me, these guys are fun."

"Yo! Danny!" Kyle tossed a football over Tom's head, and Danny reached up to catch it.

"Not in the room, guys," Danny begged.

"Not in the room," all four friends immediately chorused in silly falsettos, as if they were girls.

"You'll put somebody's eye out!" Hakeem scolded with a comic wave of his finger.

"You won't put anybody's eye out," Danny responded in a good-natured voice. "But you'll get the RA down here with security."

"Cut it out, guys!" Kyle pleaded with the others. "We've already been thrown out of the motel. If we get thrown out of Danny's dorm, we'll have to go back home and I, personally, want to see all Sweet Valley has to offer."

Tom grinned. It had been a long time since he'd had a real, old-fashioned guys' night out with a bunch of rowdy sports hounds like himself. He was totally psyched.

"Let's start with burgers," Jimmy suggested. "Then find someplace with a band. I hear the Cabana is a good place."

"I've got a better idea," Kyle said, reaching into his duffle bag and pulling out a clean shirt. "Let's go to Kitty's."

"Yeah, Kitty's! Awesome!" they all began to hoot.

Tom cleared his throat. "I don't know about . . ."

"Aw, come on," Jimmy said. "It's a great place. Good-looking girls with big . . ." The football smacked him on the head before he could finish his sentence. "Hey!" he cried out.

"Watch your mouth," Hakeem scolded. "There are ladies present."

"Where?" Jose demanded.

Hakeem pointed to Danny's picture of Isabella and Tom's picture of Elizabeth. Jose made a great pretense of looking embarrassed and turned their pictures to face the wall.

"How do you think Isabella would feel about you going to Kitty's?" Tom whispered to Danny while the four guys began to push, shove, tease, and laugh.

"About the same way Elizabeth would feel," Danny answered with a grin. "But what they don't know won't hurt them."

The phone rang, and Tom reached for it. "Hello."

"Tom?" It was Elizabeth. "What's going on over there? It sounds like you're having a party."

"Danny's friends just came in," Tom answered.

"Oh. Well, I was just calling to tell you I'm free for dinner. Any chance you could break away?"

"Oh, gee," Tom said, swallowing his guilt. "I'm sorry, but I promised Danny I'd help entertain his friends. I'd ask you to come along, but it's kind of a guys' night thing."

"No problem," she answered agreeably. "Where are you going?"

"Uh." Tom felt his cheeks turn crimson. "To a ball game," he lied.

Steven stirred his coffee and glowered into space.

"Wow! What's with the hound-dog look you've got on your face?"

Startled, Steven looked up and saw Mike

184

McAllery smiling at him. "Mind if I sit down? Or would you rather sulk by yourself?"

"What makes you think I'm sulking?" Steven pushed a chair back for Mike with his foot.

"Oh, I don't know. A guy sits by himself in a coffee shop, stirs his coffee for five minutes, and moves his lips like he's telling somebody off." Mike shrugged. "I say, it looks like he's sulking."

Steven dropped his spoon and began to blush. Mike laughed. "What's going on with the Wakefield clan? When Jessica came over to see you, she looked about as happy as you do now."

"Jessica came over to see me? When was that?" Steven felt mildly surprised. Since he hadn't heard from Jessica, he'd assumed that all was well.

"She didn't call you?" Mike signaled to the waitress to bring him a cup of coffee. "I think she wants to quit that job. But she's probably afraid to because she overheard us making our bet." He laughed knowingly. "She doesn't want to give me the satisfaction of winning."

"I'll call her," Steven said, making a mental note to check on Jessica. Bet with Mike or no bet, he didn't want her to stick with something if it was making her unhappy. If he had to spend some time helping Mike restore cars—that was fine. It wasn't as if he and Billie were spending a whole lot of time together.

"Don't call her," Mike said with a yawn, as if nothing to do with Jessica or anyone else concerned him very much. "She might not like the job, but she likes crushing me. This way, she's got something to think about besides that professor guy."

Steven returned Mike's droopy-lidded stare. Not only was McAllery right on target about Jessica, he seemed to be reading Steven's face like a book.

"So what's bugging you, man?" Mike asked bluntly when the waitress put down his coffee.

"Billie. She's on some kick where she wants to play the guitar all the time."

Mike nodded. "I hear her practicing when I'm out by the pool. She's good."

"What do you know about music?" Steven asked in an antagonistic tone.

Mike laughed. "I don't know much about music. But I know what I like. Whatever she's doing, it sounds good to me."

"What she's doing is wasting her time," Steven snapped. He closed his mouth and clenched his teeth so tightly, he felt the muscles in his jawline pop. Why was he trying to talk about this with Mike McAllery? Mike was a good guy and probably Steven's best friend at this point. But Mike was a perpetual adolescent.

"Anybody ever tell you you're a control freak?" Mike said casually.

"Yeah. So what?"

"So, some people resent being controlled."

"I'm not trying to control Billie," Steven said.

"Aren't you?"

"No. I'm trying to get her to . . ."

"To do it your way," Mike finished. "Billie's a grown woman and she's got to make her own decisions. Why does that bother you?"

Steven glanced out the window at the passing traffic and took some deep breaths. "Maybe because she's deciding she's in love with somebody else. We used to want all the same things. But now there's this guy Chas in the picture, and I think he's influencing her decisions."

There, he'd said it. He waited for Mike to laugh it off, deny it, and tell him he was crazy.

But Mike didn't answer immediately. He squinted at the ceiling and scratched the underside of his chin while he considered that. "Nah," he said finally. "I can't see it. You and Billie are too good together."

For some reason, even though he thought Mike McAllery was spoiled, vain, and irresponsible, his assessment made Steven feel better. Mike might not know much about music, but he knew about women.

"What should I do?" Steven asked.

"Calm down," Mike advised. He waved his hand indifferently. "Chill out. Give her a little space. Don't argue with her. Let her do what she wants. You've probably overreacted and she's spooked. Be supportive. Be patient. Be still. And let her come back to you."

Steven rubbed his hand over his own chin. That was exactly what had happened. He'd reacted. She'd reacted back. And the situation had taken on a life of its own. "Okay," he said. "From here on in, I'm not going to say one critical thing. Not one. I'm going to be Mr. Sensitive. Mr. Supportive. Mr. Warm and Fuzzy."

Mike laughed and signaled the waitress. "Could Mr. Warm and Fuzzy and I get a refill?"

# Chapter Fourteen

"I heard the end of your lesson," Chas said as Billie came out of Mr. Guererro's room. "You sound great." He held out his arm. "Look! Goose bumps."

Billie smiled. "Wow! I think that's better than applause."

Chas laughed. "So, are you practicing your Spanish?"

She shook her head. "Nope, I'm afraid to. It might be bad luck."

"You're getting superstitious? Where's the practical, hardheaded Billie Winkler I used to know?"

"She changed her major to music." Billie laughed.

"You're kidding?"

She shook her head. "I just filled out the paperwork with Mr. Guererro."

"So even if you don't win the competition, you're going for it?"

She nodded. "Yeah. I haven't told Steven yet.

Or my parents. Steven's going to go ballistic. And my parents . . ." Billie didn't know what her parents would think. They were both very cultured people. But they'd thoroughly discussed Billie's education and agreed that work was probably going to be a necessity for Billie, and music was a very risky career choice.

Still, she knew her parents believed that college wasn't meant to be strictly vocational training for a profession. That cultural enrichment was at least as important as academics. But she knew they'd definitely have very serious reservations about the wisdom of her changing majors at this time.

"When are you going to tell Steven?"

"After the competition," she answered. "I can't handle a lot of arguments and criticism between now and then. I've only got four more days to prepare." Billie reached into her large shoulder tote bag and removed her calendar. Her fingers rapidly flipped the pages as she prepared to see if she could squeeze a few more hours of practice in somewhere.

A notation caught her eye and she frowned. Hmm. She mentally began counting *twenty-five . . . twenty-six . . . twenty-seven . . . twenty-eight . . . twenty-nine . . .* No wonder she felt so emotional. Her period was due any minute.

Chas cleared his throat. "Billie, I know Steven doesn't like me very much, but would it help at all if I talked to him?"

Billie closed her calendar and shook her head. "No. I don't think so. And I'm sorry he's so rude to you. It's not you, you know. It's . . ."

"It's what I represent to him," Chas said.

Billie nodded unhappily. "It's what I'm going to represent to him too." A major surge of anger at Steven welled up so strongly, it threatened to choke her.

"Bruce! Would you please take off this stupid blindfold? I feel like a hostage."

"Just a few more steps," Bruce said, guiding her up the sidewalk with his hands on her shoulders. "I bought you something, and I want it to be a surprise."

Lila clicked her tongue against her front teeth in irritation. Good grief. Sometimes Bruce was as weird as Winston Egbert. "Well, hurry up because I just *know* people are staring at me. I feel so stupid."

"Well, you won't feel stupid when you see your present," Bruce said. "And heeeeere we are." He untied the scarf, waved it in the air with a flourish, and then bowed low, holding out his arm as if inviting her to look at something wondrous.

Lila frowned. She was staring into the greasy window of a doughnut shop. Hanging in the window was a pink waitress uniform with a bright pink ribbon on the shoulder. "I don't get it."

Bruce straightened up and grinned. "Step back a few feet," he instructed.

Lila backed up and shrugged. "I still don't get it."

"Look up."

Lila lifted her eyes and her jaw fell open. There was a new awning over the door, and it said LILA'S FRESH DOUGHNUTS. "Is this some kind of a joke?"

Bruce put an arm around her shoulders and squeezed. "Lila! I bought the place for you. It's yours."

"You bought me a doughnut shop?"

"Nothing's too good for my girl."

Lila turned and studied his face, looking for some signs of mental impairment. Bruce had been a little weird lately. Attentive almost to a fault. But this made no sense at all. "Bruce, why would I want a doughnut shop? Especially an old one with a greasy window."

Bruce took her hand and led her up the street. "Look!" He pointed toward the IceHouse. "What do you see?"

Lila raised her brows. "I see a lot of people going into a run-down old bar."

"Exactly!" Bruce said. "And why aren't they going to Mulberry Tavern? Or Houndstooth? Those are way more upscale."

Lila shrugged. "I don't know why."

"Because downscale is in, upscale is out."

"Say that again."

"Look. I went to the library today and read some articles on restaurants and bars. This is the trend. This is what's hip and what's in. With you and me behind this thing, Lila's Doughnuts could turn into the hottest hangout in the country. All those people who go to the IceHouse—the artists, the activists, the bikers—they'll come to Lila's too. And it'll be your own business. No Mr. Farley to yell at you or throw me out."

Suddenly Lila pictured herself as the center of attention and prime mover and shaker of a bohemian college hangout. She would have a business and an identity and something to call her own.

She looked at Bruce, and her heart began to feel strange and kind of achy. She'd never felt so touched in her life. In his own strange way, Bruce Patman had just given her everything she had ever wanted.


"Hi! Ready for another fun night at Kitty's?" Glenda asked when Elizabeth entered the staff lounge. She sat at the rickety table provided for the wait staff in the kitchen, playing with the remains of a club sandwich.

Elizabeth had entered the building through the back employees-only entrance. She hitched her thumbs in her back pockets. "Actually I'm quitting. I was going to tell you Saturday night, but it was so busy I thought I'd wait until tonight."

Glenda drained her cup of coffee and grimaced. "Do what you have to do, but *please* stay through tonight's shift. I'm still three girls short and it's a zoo out there. I think there's a playoff game on TV or something. The place is packed."

"No problem," Elizabeth agreed. "I wouldn't leave you shorthanded."

Glenda stood up. "Thanks. Think you could handle two stations?"

193

Elizabeth hesitated. She'd had more than enough of the losers at Kitty's, but knowing she could walk out and not look back suddenly made it all bearable. "No problem." Elizabeth smiled, taking the last headband from the prop box. "See you outside."

Glenda left, and Elizabeth let out a squeak of irritation when one of the ears broke off her headband. This happened more often than not, and the women kept an emergency bottle of glue in the drawer. She removed the band and had begun gluing it when the door opened and Mr. O'Connor walked in. "I'm hearing good things about you, Elizabeth," he said with a smile that looked slightly off center. "Glenda says you're a real team player. She says you really go beyond the call of duty."

Elizabeth forced herself to smile back. "Glenda's very nice," she said.

He came over and stood too close to her. "Can I help you with that?" he asked.

Elizabeth could smell liquor on his breath, and she pulled slightly away. "No thanks," she answered, putting the band on her head.

He reached out, and she jumped slightly.

"I'm just trying to adjust your ear," he said in an amused voice. "Relax."

Elizabeth began to feel uneasy. "Thanks. Well, uh, I'd better get to work." She waited for him to move out of her way, but he didn't.

"You don't need to hurry," he said, his eyes turning slightly fuzzy.

"There's a pretty big crowd out there," she

194

said. "I think I should get to my station."

He stepped a little closer. It was so obvious that he was about to try to kiss her that Elizabeth couldn't help reacting. Instinctively she put her hand on his chest and shoved. Hard. "Leave me alone," she cried.

Mr. O'Connor gaped at her. "What's with you?"

Elizabeth didn't bother to answer. She left the lounge and stalked out toward the busing station, where Glenda was sorting silverware. She was upset and her face must have shown it, because Glenda took one look and lifted a knowing eyebrow. "I meant to warn you about that." She turned back to the silverware. "He's drunk and when he's drunk, he's like an octopus."

"He's disgusting," Elizabeth said, taking a stack of napkins from the shelf.

"No argument there," Glenda said pleasantly. "Come on. Help me set up station two."

Elizabeth followed Glenda through the restaurant. She'd never seen it so crowded. And it had never been so loud.

"Whoa!" a young man shouted in mock fear as they moved toward him. "I'm about to get run over by the double-D train."

"Yeah. But what a way to go!" another guy at the table joked.

The table of five erupted into coarse male laughter. All were college age, wearing jeans or shorts and T-shirts.

"Just ignore them," Glenda instructed.

"Bet those things get heavy after a while," said a tall guy with a turned-up nose, freckles, and a baseball cap. "Want me to rub your back?"

"So much for the all-American boy," Elizabeth muttered angrily.

"No thanks," Glenda said, refusing to appear ruffled by the rude remarks about her body.

"What about you?" the boy said to Elizabeth. "I give a great back rub."

Elizabeth stacked plates and kept her mouth shut.

"Whoaaa. They're not speaking to us."

"Maybe they didn't understand the question," the second guy suggested. He wore a neon pink muscle shirt.

"Maybe not," the freckle-faced boy agreed. "You know what they say, the bigger the bra size, the smaller the brain."

Elizabeth started toward them, and Glenda put a restraining hand on her arm. "Just go to another station. I'll handle this."

"Nobody should have to handle this," Elizabeth said angrily.

"I agree," Glenda said. "But I need the paycheck, so I have no choice. Go to another station. Okay?"

Elizabeth turned away, so angry she was almost in tears. This was the end. As much as she wanted to support Glenda, she couldn't take any more. She was out of here.

She turned abruptly and bumped into someone who apologized immediately. She looked up to murmur something about it being all right, and drew in her breath with a shocked gasp instead.

His eyes bulged.

Her jaw fell open.

"Elizabeth?"

"Tom?"

"What are *you* doing here?" they both demanded at the same time.

Tom's eyes dropped to her chest and he swayed slightly on his heels. He shook his head, as if he'd just taken a blow to the jaw and was trying to get his bearings.

Elizabeth threw down her tray. Silverware clattered in every direction and glasses shattered. The tremendous noise brought all the loud conversation and laughter in the restaurant to a halt. There was a hushed, expectant pause. "You told me you were going to a ball game!" she shouted, too furious to care about who heard her. "You lied to me!"

"Look who's talking!" he sputtered. "What are you doing in a place like this?"

"I'm working on a story. And while we're on the subject, what are *you* doing in a place like this?" she countered.

"Story?" he said, ignoring her question. "What story? I don't know about any story!" He waved his fists in the air. "When are you going to stop going behind my back and become a team player? I'm the general manager at WSVU, and if you're going to work on a story—you clear it with me first." He took her arm and moved her toward the door. "Come on. You don't belong in here."

Elizabeth wrenched her arm away. "*Nobody* belongs in here. You know, women wouldn't work in places like this if men wouldn't patronize them."

Elizabeth saw Danny sitting at a table, trying hard to hide behind his menu. She reached down and snatched it away. "Don't you try to hide from me, Danny Wyatt." Danny slumped down in his chair, embarrassed.

"Look at me," she commanded, thrusting out her chest. "Everybody get a good, long look."

Danny turned away with a mortified expression on his face. So did his friends.

"What's the matter? All of a sudden it's not so funny, is it? It's not so entertaining. No. It's crude, exploitative, and demeaning . . . and you're all responsible. Not me. Not the other girls. You! The customers. The men who come here for the sole purpose of ogling women's bodies."

"Hey, watch your language," a male voice warned. Mr. O'Connor appeared at Elizabeth's elbow. "This is a legitimate food and drink establishment. We're not in the adult entertainment business."

"Oh, really?" Elizabeth asked. "Then you won't mind if I dispense with these?" She snatched the band off her head and threw her kitty ears at him. The headband bounced off the chest of his cheap, loud Hawaiian shirt. "And you won't mind if I dispense with these, too. She reached up under her shirt, into the push-up bra, and removed the two pads she'd placed in the cups. She pulled them out, deflating her bust, and threw them into the air.

Several people laughed.

"You're fired!" Mr. O'Connor said, bending down to pick up the pads and hide them in his pockets.

"For what? Not having a big bust?"

"No, for being insubordinate and rude to a customer."

"*I* haven't been insubordinate or rude to a customer," Glenda said. "Are you going to fire me too?" With that, she reached under her tight T-shirt and maneuvered around beneath it. To Elizabeth's amazement, she produced two large pads. Glenda too had been wearing foam supports that bulked up her figure.

"What about me!" Tyra said, stepping forward. "Are you going to let me go?" She reached under her shirt.

The next thing Elizabeth knew, most of the waitresses were removing foam, tissue paper, and even some gel-filled breast implants from beneath their shirts and tossing them into the air like confetti.

Suddenly most of the busty waitresses at Kitty's looked like attractive girls with ordinary figures.

There was a long silence. Elizabeth watched the faces of the men in the restaurant. Some looked amused. Some looked shocked. Some looked disappointed. And some looked just plain embarrassed. They stared down at the tabletops, unable to meet the eyes of their friends.

The silence went on and on, becoming more

and more uncomfortable, until suddenly someone began to applaud.

It was Tom. He was on his feet and applauding.

Danny stood up next to him and began clapping too.

More hands joined in the applause, and Elizabeth saw two of the girls clapping. Their faces looked grim, but relieved. As if they were glad that somebody had finally had the courage and the nerve to speak up without fear of looking uncool.

There were several squeaks and rumbles as the four big guys with Danny and Tom pushed back their chairs and stood, joining in the applause.

The table behind Elizabeth began to applaud. Then three tables in station seven.

Glenda came over and took her hand. They lifted their hands in a victory gesture. All the female customers began to cheer, and the thundering applause grew even stronger.

Elizabeth had thought she couldn't get any support. She'd thought she was alone. But she was wrong. Women could work together to make things better for each other. All it took was solidarity, a few strong women, and some really great guys like Tom and Danny.

This was going to make a great story.

# Chapter
# Fifteen

"Billie? Billie, is there anything I can do?"

The only answer was a choking sound followed by a flush. Steven winced slightly and went to the kitchen, feeling more alarmed and disturbed than before. Billie had been sick every single morning for the last four days.

He'd tried to be sympathetic, but when he'd suggested yesterday that she see a doctor, Billie had bitten his head off, insisting that it was just stress.

Stress? What stress? Steven had gone out of his way to make sure Billie's life was as stress free as possible. Just as he'd promised Mike. He'd been unfailingly supportive, warm, and fuzzy.

Had it worked?

No.

Over the last four days Billie had become increasingly irritable. Increasingly angry. And increasingly sick.

If stress was making her sick, it was the stress of the competition. Thankfully it would all be over this afternoon. He didn't know how much more of this he could take.

Steven poured himself a cup of coffee, trying to emotionally disconnect from her distress. How could she insist that music was what she wanted when the strain of it made her so sick? She'd never been queasy or vomited before this guitar thing.

Billie appeared at the kitchen door and threw Steven a dark look, as if challenging him to say a word. He said nothing, simply wrapping some ice from the freezer in a dish towel and breaking it against the counter. "Chipped ice will keep you from getting dehydrated," he said softly.

"Thank you," she said in a subdued tone, taking the glass of chipped ice he'd prepared.

"You're welcome," he responded stiffly.

She sat on a stool and put a chip in her mouth, taking some deep breaths. Her eyes looked everywhere but at him. "You said you wanted to get to the auditorium early. Want me to drive you to campus?" he asked.

"No," she said.

"How are you going to get there?"

"Chas said he'd pick me up."

Steven rubbed his head in both hands. Chas would pick her up. Chas says this. Chas thinks that. All he heard about was Chas, Chas, Chas.

The stress of Billie's relationship with Steven wasn't what was making her sick. It wasn't the stress of preparing for the competition. It was the stress of secrecy.

"Billie." He sighed. "If you think you're doing me a favor by lying to me, you're not."

"What are you talking about?" she demanded.

He lifted his head. "If you're in love with somebody else, I'd rather know about it. Just tell me and quit making yourself sick and me miserable."

"What?"

"I'm not a complete idiot. I know what's going on. You're in love with Chas, aren't you?"

"I'm not in love with Chas," she cried angrily. "What would make you think something crazy like that?"

"Because something's wrong," Steven said, standing up and beginning to pace. "I thought it was me and the way I was acting. But I've been really supportive about this music stuff for the last few days and I'm getting nowhere. If I try to talk to you about anything, I get my head bitten off." He could hear the anger and impatience in his voice, but he couldn't help it. "So if you're not in love with somebody else, what can possibly be wrong?"

Billie said nothing.

Steven threw up his hands and stomped out of the kitchen. "See? This is impossible."

"Stop it!" she shouted tearfully, jumping off the bar stool. "Just stop it."

He whirled around. "Stop *what*?" he yelled

at the top of his voice. "Stop loving you?"

She dropped the glass of ice and covered her face with her hands. "You're making me crazy!" She began to sob.

"How? Why? What am I doing? What's got you so bugged?" he yelled in frustration. "What?"

Billie continued to weep, her shoulders shaking.

"I know you're unhappy, but how can I fix it if I don't know the problem?"

She lifted her red, tear-streaked face. "I think I'm pregnant!" she yelled.

"What?"

"I think I'm pregnant," she said again, shouting even louder. "There. Happy now?" With that, she burst into tears again.

He'd never actually had a bucket of cold water thrown on him, but he knew now what it would feel like.

*Pregnant?* Billie thought she was *pregnant?*

Steven didn't know whether to take her in his arms or kick a hole in the wall.

Tom saw Elizabeth coming out of the library and ran to catch up with her, falling into step beside her. "Hi there. You look familiar. Haven't I seen you on a calendar?"

Elizabeth stopped and made a fairly good attempt to step on his toes.

"Peace. Peace!" he said with a laugh, doing some fancy stepping to avoid the toes of her boots.

She grinned and settled for elbowing him in the ribs. "Still hanging with Danny's friends?"

Tom smiled. "They left yesterday. They weren't a bad bunch of guys. And they thought you were great." He reached into his pocket and pulled out a piece of paper. "They asked me to give you this."

"What is it?"

"Their phone numbers. They said I wasn't nearly good enough for you, and if you ever broke up with me, they'd all like to hear from you."

Elizabeth threw back her head and laughed.

"And that's not all. I just got a call from Glenda at the station. Your story on the female solidarity issue got picked up by one of the national wire services. As a result, some lawyer called Glenda and offered to sue the Kitty Corporation on behalf of all the waitresses for sexual harassment and discrimination. The Kitty Corporation got so nervous, they sold the restaurant. It's going to reopen next week as an upscale steak and lobster restaurant. And guess who bought it?"

"Who?"

"Fowler Enterprises."

Elizabeth's brows rose in surprise. "That's great."

"And guess who's going to manage it?"

"Mr. O'Connor," Elizabeth joked.

"No . . . Glenda."

Elizabeth adjusted her baseball cap and tightened her ponytail in the back. "Cool. I'll tell Amy Briar to call her. I don't think Glenda cares what a girl looks like as long as she does a good job."

"So now that you're no longer a working girl, can I talk you into dinner tonight?"

"Only if you'll come with me to a guitar competition this afternoon. Billie's performing."

"Sounds like fun. I love guitar music."

"We can go to dinner after."

"So it's a date?" he asked in a doubtful tone. His eyes grew large in comic surprise. "We really have a date? Finally?"

"We really have a date," she confirmed with a laugh. "Unless I catch you hanging out in a girly bar."

"And unless I catch you working in one," he retorted.

"Nancy!" Lila signaled to the high school girl who worked behind the counter at Lila's Doughnuts. "Would you bring my friend some crullers and a cup of coffee?"

"Nothing for me," Jessica corrected. "I'm cashless until I get my next paycheck."

Lila waved an airy hand. "It's on the house."

Jessica smiled back. "Gee, thanks, Lila. That's really nice."

"We working girls have to look out for each other," she said.

"Yeah, but you've got to make some money."

Lila waved her hand again. "As soon as we get the cappuccino machine and computers in here, I'll be swimming in money. Right now I'm just trying to build a following."

"Ms. Fowler," Nancy said, coming over to the table with a plate of chocolate-filled doughnuts. "We don't have any more crullers. You donated them all to the shelter."

"These are fine," Jessica said, taking the plate and the coffee from her and attacking a doughnut.

There was a burst of laughter and chatter, and Lila sat up straighter as Danny, Isabella, Denise, Winston, Alex, and Noah came in the door. "Welcome to Lila's Doughnuts," Lila cried light-heartedly.

Isabella looked around and nodded. "This place has definite possibilities," she said.

"Absolutely," Denise agreed. "And we'll get all the Thetas to hang out here. The art students will love it too," she added. "It's got a real funky downtown look."

"I thought we'd have a counter of computers against that wall so people can do homework or surf the net while they hang out," Lila said.

Everybody began pulling chairs up to the table, and Denise produced a sketch pad from her backpack. "Let's do some preliminary designs," she suggested.

"Now, we don't want to get too fancy," Lila warned. "Or we'll lose the shabby-chic quality that makes this place what it is."

"Definitely," Denise agreed, her pencil flying over the page. "But if you put the computers on a beat-up Formica counter with red stools every few feet, you'd keep the same look as the rest of the place."

"I know where you could get another counter," Isabella said. "They're tearing down an old coffee shop on Twenty-second Street."

Soon everybody was talking at once. Making suggestions. Eating doughnuts. Sipping coffee and having a great time.

"This thing could be huge," Winston said. "Real huge."

"What are you going to do with the huge amounts of money you'll be making?" Denise asked.

"Bruce and I talked about that. We thought we'd make it a nonprofit organization," Lila responded. "All the profits will go to the Sweet Valley Coalition for Battered Women."

The table was silent. Then Isabella smiled warmly. "That's the greatest thing I've ever heard."

Lila smiled, pleased to have earned Isabella's approval. She'd always been slightly in awe of the sophisticated older girl.

Winston lifted his coffee cup, as if making a toast. "To Lila the philanthropist," he said.

Everyone at the table lifted their coffee cups and clinked them together.

Steven paced up and down outside the bathroom door. He checked his watch. What was taking so long?

As soon as Billie had made her tearful announcement, he'd mobilized—getting her to calm down, assuring her that a late period wasn't necessarily a sign of pregnancy, and running out to the pharmacy for a home pregnancy kit.

Together they'd read the instructions, and then Billie had gone into the bathroom to do the test.

He knocked softly on the door with one knuckle. "Billie? Are you okay?"

The door opened, and Billie walked out like someone in shock. She didn't have to say a word. It was obvious from her face that the result was positive. Billie sank down on the couch and buried her face in her hands.

Steven felt his body go numb again. His fingertips and toes felt icy and his lips had lost all sensation. But as shocked and stunned as he felt, his mind was already racing ahead—thinking and planning.

He hurried to the couch and sat down beside her, pulling Billie's hands from her face and rubbing his hands up and down her arms. They were as icy cold as his felt. "Let's not panic," he cautioned, his voice sounding surprisingly calm. "You can't be very far along. That gives us plenty of time to get ready."

"Ready?" she repeated, blinking at him. "Ready for what?"

Steven couldn't help laughing. Her mind still hadn't made all the connections. "For the baby," he explained.

The word *baby* sent a surge of adrenaline coursing through his bloodstream.

They were going to have a baby. A human

baby. In about eight months, give or take a few days, their lives were going to be turned upside down.

But with a little planning on their part, it wouldn't be catastrophic. "We'll get married as soon as possible," he said. "The baby won't arrive until next semester. We'll both take summer school classes and I'll be able to graduate a semester early. That way I can start looking for a job right away and hopefully be working by the time the baby gets here. You'll probably want to take a semester off, but we should plan on you graduating in the spring two years from now and then starting law school right away."

Billie's eyes looked blank and hollow. Steven knew it was more information than she could process in one gulp. He took her hand and squeezed it. "Billie," he said softly. "Don't worry. I love you. I'm going to take care of everything. It's going to be all right."

# Chapter
# Sixteen

Bruce bustled into Lila's Doughnuts. "The seamstress isn't through yet," he called out to Lila. He grabbed a paper coffee cup and helped himself from the industrial-size urn behind the counter.

"Darn!" Lila sat at her own table in the corner, surrounded by Danny, Isabella, Winston, Denise, and Jessica. "I'm having my uniform remade in pink satin," she told them.

"Wow! *Trés chic*," Isabella commented.

"I'm going to wear it all the time," Lila said. "It'll be like my signature."

Bruce hurried over and kissed Lila on the cheek before sitting down at the table with his coffee. "So what did I miss?" He reached for a packet of sugar.

"We were just talking about fund-raising and Lila's Doughnuts," Lila answered. "We need a major kickoff event that will let people know who we are and what we're doing. I called the newspapers and talked with some of the lifestyle editors about it. They said it was a great concept, but the only way to get newspaper coverage would be if we had some kind of event."

"So now we're trying to think of what Lila can do," Isabella said. "I suggested a bake-off."

Denise wrinkled her nose. "Too old-fashioned. And besides, I don't know how to bake anything."

"Me neither," Jessica said.

"Pass," Winston said.

They all looked at Bruce. "Hey! Don't look at me. I don't know how to bake anything either. The only people around here who know how to bake anything are Nancy and Bart. And all they can make are doughnuts."

"A dance?" Jessica suggested.

"We just had a sock hop," Isabella said. "I don't know if we could get people excited about another dance this soon."

"What about an auction?" Denise suggested.

"Been done twice already this year," Danny answered.

Lila let out her breath in a long, weary sigh. "I can't think of anything else. Fund-raising is not as simple as it seems."

"Well, hey," Bruce said. "Even if you don't come up with a great fund-raising idea, you'll still be donating all the proceeds from the doughnut shop."

"What proceeds?" Nancy said under her breath

as she moved behind Bruce's chair to put another plate of doughnuts down on the table. "What she doesn't give to the Sweet Valley Coalition for Battered Women, she gives to her friends."

"Hey! When we get this place launched, the money will come rolling in," Lila insisted optimistically.

Bruce reached for a doughnut and took a satisfied bite. Yep. The old Bruce Patman brain hadn't failed him. This doughnut shop had been his greatest idea. It had taken him a long time to erase the haunted, unhappy look Lila had worn in the months after Tisiano's death. And once he'd gotten her emotionally stabilized after that, her old man had come in and let the air out of her ego. But good old Uncle Bruce had come up with the answer. Who'd have thought that all Lila Fowler really wanted out of life was a greasy doughnut shop of her very own?

Jessica and Lila were chattering happily with Isabella and Denise when suddenly Jessica let out a little yip of panic. "Oh, no! Look at the time. I'm going to be late." She jumped to her feet, grabbed her purse, and waved good-bye to everyone.

"Have a good day at work," Lila called as Jessica raced to the door. Jessica turned her head to answer when the little bell over the door tinkled and a man came walking in.

Jessica plowed right into him, and the man went down with a loud crash and a bellow of alarm. Bruce, Lila, Isabella, and Danny jumped to their feet and ran to his aid.

"I'm all right," he insisted as they hauled him to his feet. "I'm all right."

Jessica lingered just long enough to make sure everything was fine before racing out the door.

The man brushed himself off, and Bruce batted the lint and dust from the sleeve of his jacket. "I'm really, really sorry," he said. "Are you sure you're okay? Would you like to sit down?"

"No, no," the man said in a good-humored tone. "I just came in to pick up a dozen doughnuts and—" He broke off and stared at Lila. "Say. Are you an actress or something?"

Lila smiled in a pleased way. "No. Why do you ask?"

"You look familiar," the man said. "Have we met before?"

"I don't think so," Lila responded. "My name is Lila Fowler."

"Fowler . . . Fowler . . ." the man mused. He snapped his fingers. "Oh, I know. You're the heiress whose husband died in the Jet Ski accident in Italy. I read all about it. So I guess you're the Lila of Lila's Doughnuts."

Lila's eyes dropped to her feet, and Bruce felt like kicking the man he'd just helped off the floor. There had been a lot of newspaper publicity about the death of Lila's husband and her return to Sweet Valley. After all, an eighteen-year-old countess from California made a very romantic and tragic figure.

214

Clearly it was Bruce's duty to get rid of this loser before he said something that would totally bum Lila out. "I'm sorry," he said in as cold a tone as he could muster. "But we're not really a doughnut shop."

The man's brows rose in surprise. "But . . ."

"We're a nonprofit organization for battered women," Lila explained.

The man put his hands over his breast, as if he were incredibly moved. "What a beautiful gesture. She's rich. She's beautiful. She's a countess. And on top of everything else, she's a selfless benefactress of the less fortunate in our community."

Bruce thought he might be sick, but Lila looked oddly happy.

"Benefactress," she repeated in a low tone. "I like that."

Bruce zipped behind the counter, snagged the remaining few doughnuts, and popped them into the bag. Then he plastered a big smile on his face that was as phony as the guy's. "Here. Please take this and our apologies for the inconvenience." He thrust the bag into the man's hand and gently pushed him toward the door.

"This was truly a lucky day," the man said in a voice of breathless admiration as Bruce propelled him out to the sidewalk.

"Yeah. Whatever. Thanks for dropping in."

The door closed and the little bell tinkled. Bruce shut it firmly. "We're out of doughnuts anyway. And we've got work to do in here. So let's

215

make sure we don't have any more windbags blowing in."

Jessica ran down the street, her heels clattering on the pavement. Taylor's was only a few blocks away, but she had less than five minutes to get there. It was at least a ten-minute walk in sneakers. Fifteen in the three-inch heels she had on.

Her shoulder bag swung wildly, bumping against her hip and the passersby who narrowly missed her as she hurtled toward Taylor's.

She couldn't believe she'd managed to lose track of the time. Mr. Farley was looking for a chance to fire her. In fact, he was just waiting for an excuse. If she was late one more time, he'd boot her for sure.

Oddly enough, she felt a tear trickle down her cheek.

Taylor's was a crummy store, but she didn't want to be fired. She'd begun to think of herself as a professional. To be dismissed for something as childish as chronic lateness seemed unbearably embarrassing and demoralizing.

Maybe she was growing up—finally.

She had a vision of Val and Mike sipping beers somewhere, talking about her.

Val would say something very nice, but nonetheless, she would shake her head and convey the impression that Jessica just wasn't up to the demands of the professional retail business.

Mike would roar with laughter, get weeks of

free labor from Steven because of her, and on top of it all, tease her unmercifully. Mike loved nothing better than taking Jessica down a peg or two. The only person who would be happier about her dismissal than Mr. Farley was Mike McAllery.

A motorcycle roared up, and Mike McAllery bumped along the curb beside her. *Speak of the devil,* she thought.

"Where you going, beautiful?"

She didn't answer.

"Late again?" he asked.

She forced herself to stop. "No," she lied, thinking quickly. "I left the store a little while ago, and I forgot my wallet on the counter. I want to hurry back before it's stolen."

"Hop on," he said cheerfully, handing her the spare helmet.

Jessica glanced at her watch. She had exactly three minutes now. She grabbed the helmet, tucked her long blond hair up into it, and threw a leg over the seat. She tucked her purse up underneath her arm and wrapped her arms around his waist.

She could feel his hard abdominal muscles tighten as the bike roared out into traffic. Jessica closed her eyes. Mike was a fearless rider, and soon she felt them weaving in and out of traffic—careening from one lane to the next and speeding up to beat yellow lights.

*I'd rather be dead than fired and ridiculed,* she told herself, fighting the impulse to tap Mike on the shoulder and beg him to slow down. Moments later they screeched to a stop.

"Want me to wait?" he asked as she climbed off the bike and handed him the helmet.

"No, thanks," she said with a laugh. "I'll be here quite a while. I'm actually just starting my shift."

"You mean . . ."

"That's right, Mr. McAllery. You've been had. You could have won your bet if you hadn't given me a ride."

He laughed and shook his head. But he didn't look mad or disappointed. He scratched his stubbly chin and shrugged. "Easy come, easy go. That goes for cars, money, and women."

"And ex-husbands," she retorted. "Toodle-oo!" She fluttered her fingers in a mocking wave and pirouetted. Then she took several long strides toward the front door. She was at work with two seconds to spare. She almost hoped Mr. Farley would come bearing down on her with a watch in his hand. It would be so nice to point out that she wasn't late after all.

But there was no Mr. Farley to greet her. In fact, there was no one in the front section of the store at all. She looked around, confused. What was going on? Where was everybody?

She took a few steps farther into the store, until she was standing in the middle of Men's Wear. "Hello?" she said in a tentative voice.

It was so strange, she began to feel afraid.

Maybe the store was being robbed. Maybe all the employees were tied up and locked in a storage room.

She began to back up slowly, looking all around the silent first floor. Even the escalators had come to a stop. *I'm getting out of here,* she thought.

But before she could act, she backed into somebody and let out a scream.

She whirled and found herself face to face with a security guard. "What's going on?" she demanded. "Where is everybody? You scared me to death."

"Sorry I scared you. I was supposed to be at the door, directing everybody to go upstairs, but I had to check on something in the back."

"Upstairs?" she repeated in confusion. "Why is everybody upstairs?"

"Staff meeting," he said.

"Now?"

He shrugged. "All I know is that I'm supposed to send everybody upstairs. You're the last one."

Jessica rushed over to the escalator and began climbing the stationary stairs. This was weird. Really weird. When she reached the second floor, Jessica saw a large knot of people gathered in the spacious area that separated evening clothes and lingerie. She hurried to join the others.

As she approached they all turned briefly to see who was joining them, and then turned their attention back to the man who stood in the center of the group.

"What's going on?" Jessica whispered to the girl who managed the inventory lists in the office.

"We're closed," the girl whispered back.

"What!"

"Quiet, please," the man said, holding up his hand. "As I'm trying to explain, Taylor's is no longer in business. It was acquired by Fowler Enterprises several months ago. Fowler Enterprises is closing the store today, and you are all dismissed as of now."

A loud commotion arose, and the man waved his hand. "Please. Please," he begged. "Let me finish."

The crowd became silent. Across the room Jessica watched Val Tripler's intent look. These jobs were important to a lot of people who worked here. They depended on them for their livelihoods. She saw Mr. Farley, and suddenly she didn't hate him anymore. She felt sorry for him. He'd worked at Taylor's for years. And now he was out of a job.

"All permanent and/or longtime employees will receive generous severance packages. Those close to retirement will receive their full pensions."

Jessica began to feel better.

"Why all the secrecy?" one employee asked. "Why weren't we informed that Fowler Enterprises had acquired the store several months ago?"

"Because Fowler Enterprises was attempting to acquire several adjoining properties in order to build a complex of luxury apartments. They were afraid that if it were known, real-estate prices would inflate beyond a reasonable purchase price. Therefore it was necessary to maintain the illusion that the store was still a viable merchandising corporation."

Suddenly it all made sense to Jessica. The old stock. The dusty merchandise. The slowness with which shelves were restocked. If a store was just pretending to be in business, it naturally wouldn't want to spend a lot of money on inventory.

"Employees who need help finding new jobs will find that Fowler Enterprises offers an extensive range of out-placement services. That means we'll help you find new jobs." He held up a stack of leaflets. "I have the information here for anyone who's interested. Your checks will be mailed to you. And I suppose there is nothing else to say besides have a nice day and enjoy your afternoon off."

The crowd began to drift away. Some people looked stunned. Some looked happy. And some looked as if they still couldn't take it all in.

Personally, Jessica felt jubilant. She hadn't quit. And she hadn't been fired. She'd been rendered obsolete—which meant she didn't have to work here anymore. Steven wouldn't have to work for Mike. And nobody could say she hadn't done a good job.

She turned, intending to return immediately to the doughnut shop and tell Lila what had happened—that her father's company had owned Taylor's Department Store all along.

It was pretty funny when you thought about it.

Once outside, she noticed that Mike was still sitting on his motorcycle, reading the paper.

"What are you doing?"

He smiled. "I thought you might get fired. So I waited around to give you a lift home."

"Well, guess again," she bantered. "I didn't get fired. And I didn't quit."

"Then that was the shortest shift in the history of work. That must be some union you're in."

"Actually, the store is out of business."

Mike looked surprised. "Taylor's is out of business?"

She nodded. "That's right. No more Taylor's."

He pinched at his earlobe and grimaced. "Poor Val," he muttered.

Jessica felt another irrational stab of jealousy. Why was he worrying about Val, and not about her? She forced herself to be reasonable. Val supported herself with her job. Jessica didn't. So it was only natural that he'd be more concerned about her than Jessica. "Full-time employees are getting good severance," she said. "And Fowler Enterprises will help them get new jobs."

Mike nodded. "So . . . can I take you home or what?"

"Or what," she said, not quite forgiving him for expressing so much interest in Val's welfare.

He grinned, as if he could read her mind. "Then toodle-oo," he said to *her* this time, giving her a silly flutter of his fingers before roaring off.

Jessica watched him pull out in front of a black Porsche and screech around the corner.

"He'll get himself smushed one day," a voice commented behind her.

Jessica turned and saw Val smiling at her. "How does it feel to be unemployed?" Val asked.

"It feels great to me," Jessica replied honestly. "But it probably doesn't feel so great for you. Are you going to let Fowler Enterprises help you find a new job?"

Val squinted up into the sun, as if she were thinking very hard about something. "I don't think so. At least not yet. I've had an idea for a long time now. An idea for a business. But I need a partner. Would you be interested?"

Jessica drew in her breath with a gasp. Val Tripler wanted *her* for a partner? It was the most incredibly flattering thing that had ever happened to her. "What . . . what kind of business?" she asked.

"Let's go get a cup of coffee," Val suggested. "I'll tell you all about it."

"Ms. Fowler! We meet again."

"Mr. Farley!" Lila looked up from her sketch book and blinked in surprise. Mr. Farley stood on the sidewalk outside Lila's Doughnuts and gave Lila his customary bland smile. "What are you doing here?"

"I'm here to buy a cup of coffee."

"But it's closed. I mean we're closed. I mean . . . we're renovating," she sputtered in confusion. She looked at her watch. "Besides, it's working hours."

Mr. Farley straightened his tie. "Not for me. I've been downsized."

"What?" Lila wondered if Mr. Farley were drunk.

"Rendered obsolete."

She blinked.

"Fired," he explained.

"Fired! For what?"

Mr. Farley cocked his head. "Surely you know."

"Know what?"

"About Taylor's."

"What about it?"

It was Mr. Farley who looked surprised now. "I take it your father doesn't confide in you?"

Lila was beginning to get angry. This was her doughnut shop and her sidewalk. Mr. Farley was her enemy. She didn't have to stand here talking to some insulting retail supervisor. But before she could say a word, he removed his sunglasses.

"I thought surely you were aware that your father had purchased the store."

"My father purchased Taylor's?" Lila interrupted. "When?"

"Some months ago. It's been rumored for some time."

Lila's mind was racing, casting frantically back over the last few days, trying to put things together. "But if you knew my father owned the store, why did you . . ."

"Fire you?" His bland smile grew blander. "Because I consider myself a professional. I'm proud of the work I do. And as long as I'm in charge, the people who work for me will uphold my standards or work someplace else."

*He knew exactly who you were.* Her father's words echoed through her mind. Then she pictured his laughing face.

Lila dropped the sketch pad and began running, her heart pounding in her chest. She never even stopped at the corner to look for traffic. A red Toyota narrowly missed her and a black Jeep rolled up on the sidewalk to avoid hitting the Toyota.

The driver of the Toyota angrily honked his horn, and the driver of the Jeep yelled some insult out the window. But Lila paid no attention.

"Lila! Lila, stop!" She felt a hand close over her arm and pull her to a stop. "What's the matter?"

"Let me go," she shouted angrily at Bruce.

"Where are you going?" Bruce panted. "I was watching you out the window and suddenly you took off like you'd gotten a 911 call. Do you realize you almost got killed?"

"I've got to find my father," she gasped, her rib cage heaving.

"Your father? Why? What's going on?"

"Did you know he owns Taylor's Department Store?" she demanded.

Bruce shook his head. "No. And even if he does, so what?"

"So it means he let that Farley guy humiliate his own daughter just for the sake of a business deal!" she shouted, tears streaming down her face. "And when I'd told Dad what had happened . . . he *laughed* at me. No one laughs at Lila Fowler and gets away with it. . . . Not even my own dad!"

# Chapter
## Seventeen

_____

"I can't do it," Billie gasped.

"Yes, you can," Steven insisted.

Her shaking hands fidgeted wildly at her hair. "I don't feel good. I don't want to do this. There's no point, and . . ."

"Take a deep breath," Steven instructed. They were backstage at the auditorium. Billie had called Chas and told him that Steven would drive her to the competition.

Billie inhaled.

"Take another one."

While Billie took another deep breath, Steven peered around the edge of the curtain. He saw Elizabeth and Tom sitting in the front row. And beside Tom, he saw Chas. For the first time, he was able to look at Chas and not feel threatened. He turned back to Billie. "You can do it."

Her eyes turned toward him like a panicked deer's.

"You can do it," he repeated in an urgent whisper.

"Shhhh." A backstage manager put his finger to his lips, cautioning them to be quiet, then he held up his hand, indicating that Billie should get ready to go on.

Steven leaned down and took Billie's guitar from the case. He handed it solemnly to her. "Go for it," he mouthed.

The stage manager began to gesture frantically. Steven put his hand on her shoulder and pushed gently.

Billie cast a last look over her shoulder, then walked out onstage. Steven peered out and watched the audience applaud.

She settled herself on the stool, and Steven leaned forward. She looked beautiful in the spotlight. Her neck curved gracefully like a swan's as she bent over the guitar and positioned her fingers on the strings.

Steven had only half listened to all the other players. His mind had been far too preoccupied with thoughts of Billie and the child they were about to have.

But as she began to play, the music touched his heart in a way it never had before. He saw her in a different light. She had always been smart and beautiful. But now he saw a side of her that was tender and passionate and emotional.

Billie was going to be a wonderful mother. And she would have so much to offer their child. Music wasn't a very practical career choice, but it did transform the heart and soul. It would be a wonderful hobby to share with their child.

Steven vowed to work as hard as he could—at all aspects of family life. He was going to try harder to listen. Try harder to be sensitive. Try harder in school.

If he could be half as good as a father as Billie was going to be as a mother, their child would be okay. Not just okay. Fantastic.

He closed his eyes and let the music wash over him, feeling as if his life was just beginning.

*This is going to sound mean, and I hope you'll take it the right way, but I wouldn't worry too much about winning.*

She hadn't worried about winning. She'd worried about losing. But now, she hoped with all her heart that she'd lose. It would be easier that way. Because after today, she was going to put aside the guitar—forever.

Somewhere in the last few days, she had crossed whatever invisible border separated the happy amateur from the professional.

If she couldn't be a professional, she had no interest in continuing to play for a hobby.

It was like ending a relationship. A good, clean break was a lot easier than a prolonged parting.

Her fingers flew over the strings and she played with more intensity and emotion than she'd ever played in her life. It was like kissing a lover for the last time.

Suddenly, before she knew it, she was at the end of the piece. She plucked a string, and the last note echoed through the concert hall, growing fainter and fainter until finally it was gone.

There was a stunned pause, and then the audience was on its feet. Even the judges in the front row stood.

Billie's dazed eyes searched the auditorium until she found his face. Mr. Guererro beamed at her from the fifth row. Their eyes met, and Billie felt her face crumple. Tears streamed down her cheeks and she ran from the stage, knocking over the stool in her haste.

Sobbing, she ran into the wings and threw herself against Steven's chest, dropping the guitar to the floor, where it hummed a tuneful protest.

"Billie! Billie!" Steven laughed. "Why are you crying? You did great. I think you won."

She put her arms around Steven and held on for dear life, trying to keep the pain at bay. "I know," she wept into his chest. "And it's the most awful thing that could have happened to me."

*Will Billie really win the scholarship to Spain? And if she does, what will happen to Steven . . . and their baby? Find out what Billie decides in Sweet Valley University #19,* **BROKEN PROMISES, SHATTERED DREAMS.**

## SIGN UP FOR THE SWEET VALLEY HIGH® FAN CLUB!

Hey, girls! Get all the gossip on Sweet Valley High's® most popular teenagers when you join our fantastic Fan Club! As a member, you'll get all of this really cool stuff:

- Membership Card with your own personal Fan Club ID number
- A Sweet Valley High® Secret Treasure Box
- Sweet Valley High® Stationery
- Official Fan Club Pencil (for secret note writing!)
- Three Bookmarks
- A "Members Only" Door Hanger
- Two Skeins of J. & P. Coats® Embroidery Floss with flower barrette instruction leaflet
- Two editions of *The Oracle* newsletter
- Plus exclusive Sweet Valley High® product offers, special savings, contests, and much more!

Be the first to find out what Jessica & Elizabeth Wakefield are up to by joining the Sweet Valley High® Fan Club for the one-year membership fee of only $6.25 each for U.S. residents, $8.25 for Canadian residents (U.S. currency). Includes shipping & handling.

Send a check or money order (do not send cash) made payable to "Sweet Valley High® Fan Club" along with this form to:

**SWEET VALLEY HIGH® FAN CLUB, BOX 3919-B, SCHAUMBURG, IL 60168-3919**

NAME _____
(Please print clearly)

ADDRESS _____

CITY _____ STATE _____ ZIP_____
(Required)

AGE _____ BIRTHDAY_____ / _____ / _____

*Life* after high school gets even *Sweeter!*

Jessica and Elizabeth are now freshmen at Sweet Valley University, where the motto is: Welcome to college — welcome to freedom!

### Don't miss any of the books in this fabulous new series.

| | | |
|---|---|---|
| ♥ College Girls #1 | 0-553-56308-4 | $3.50/$4.50 Can. |
| ♥ Love, Lies and<br>   Jessica Wakefield #2 | 0-553-56306-8 | |
| | | $3.50/$4.50 Can. |
| ♥ What Your Parents<br>   Don't Know #3 | 0-553-56307-6 | |
| | | $3.50/$4.50 Can. |
| ♥ Anything for Love #4 | 0-553-56311-4 | $3.50/$4.50 Can. |
| ♥ A Married Woman #5 | 0-553-56309-2 | $3.50/$4.50 Can. |
| ♥ The Love of Her Life #6 | 0-553-56310-6 | $3.50/$4.50 Can. |